It was like Taylor did something to *cause* Adriana to be out of school," Alyssa said.

Chloe rolled her eyes. "C'mon, Lyss. Taylor's not like that."

"I know you like her," said Sam reasonably, "and I understand why you're sticking up for her. But you've got to admit, Chloe, it's strange."

"She was fiddling with that weird necklace of hers," Kimmie recalled. "Maybe the crystal has powers!"

Chloe couldn't believe what she was hearing. "Seriously?"

Kimmie shrugged and poked at the macaroni and cheese on her plate. "It's possible. I mean, she is from Salem. Maybe her crystal got some of that old-time Salem magic stuck to it before Taylor moved. Maybe Taylor can't help what happens when she wears it."

POISON APPLE BOOKS

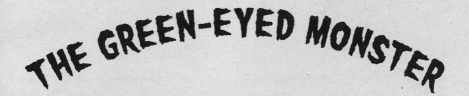

THE GREEN-EYED MONSTER

by Lisa Fiedler

POISON APPLE

SCHOLASTIC INC.

To Madeline Rose, Samuel James, and Sophia
Marie with love, and, as always, to Shannon

ISBN 978-0-545-48424-4

12 11 10 9 8 7 6 5 4 3 2 1   12 13 14 15 16 17/0

Printed in the U.S.A.   40
First printing, January 2013

CHAPTER ONE

Chloe Rawlings held her breath.

It was something she always did when she walked past the graveyard on Old Burial Hill. Maybe it was silly, but when she and her best friend, Samantha Kendall, were in first grade, Samantha's older brother, Davis, had once told them that restless spirits could rise out of their graves and possess the souls of the living as they passed by. They'd made a pact never to pass the creepy, historic cemetery without holding their breath so they couldn't be possessed.

Now that Chloe was older, she secretly reasoned that any spirit with common sense would surely find a less disgusting way to enter a person's soul than through her nasal passages. But she'd promised Sam, and she'd never broken a promise to her BFF in

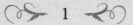

her life. And considering how tense things had been between them lately, now was definitely not the time to start. Chloe and Sam had been best buds forever and had never had so much as a cross word between them until just this week. And over silly little things, too, like where to sit in the lunchroom and which (if either) of them Jake Bailey had been smiling at in gym class.

She slid a sideways glance at Sam, who was walking beside her now, just as she did most days after school. Sam was holding her breath, too. Not that it made much difference conversation-wise, since the two hadn't uttered a word to each other since they'd left school. Ordinarily, their walks home were filled with giggly chitchat about the day, sharing thoughts about their teachers, killer homework assignments, or snooty eighth graders. But today the only thing they'd shared was awkward silence.

At the top of the hill, Chloe paused (her lungs still holding in a big gulp of cool, fresh air) to admire the scene below. Marblehead Harbor glittered in the early November sunshine. Only a few graceful sailboats remained in their moorings this time of year and an unseasonably warm breeze rippled the water's surface. It was such a familiar and beautiful

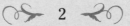

scene that it was almost enough to make her forget the horrible week she'd just had: misplacing her favorite sweater, flunking a pop quiz in pre-algebra, and, worst of all, arguing with Sam.

On any other day, they'd be pointing to the schooners and planning ahead for a "round the world" sailing adventure with their future husbands — Chloe's would be a rock star; Sam's, a brain surgeon (or possibly a dog groomer, she could never decide). Today, though, neither said a word.

Finally, Chloe couldn't take it anymore; she let out her breath in an exasperated rush. *So much for warding off the spirits,* she thought. But what she had to say was more important than ghosts, and she couldn't wait.

"I still can't believe you won't audition with me!" she blurted.

Sam turned to face her, her cheeks all puffed out with captured air, and shook her head emphatically.

"But I joined intramural dodgeball with you when you asked me to!" Chloe reminded her. "Remember?"

Rolling her eyes, Sam released her breath. "That was in third grade, Chloe! And it didn't involve me standing onstage in front of the whole school."

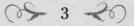

"But it did involve me wearing a jersey with the ridiculous team name on it," Chloe snapped. "I became a Darling Dodging Diva for you! When it comes to making sacrifices in the name of friendship, that's a pretty major one!"

"I didn't make up the name," said Sam. "And I'm sorry if being my best friend is such a major sacrifice!"

Chloe thought she noticed Sam's lip tremble. "That's not what I meant, and you know it," she protested. But Sam was already stomping off down the hill toward home.

Shaking her head in frustration, Chloe turned back to the nautical scene spread out below her.

"Nice view."

The voice startled Chloe.

She turned to see a girl standing behind her. For a moment, Chloe had the crazy impression that the girl was glowing, until she realized it was the sun glinting off the heart-shaped crystal charm of the choker she wore around her neck.

"Yeah, the harbor is at its prettiest this time of day," Chloe agreed.

"I'm Taylor Dunbar," said the girl, stepping closer. Her auburn hair cascaded in waves around her face,

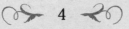

reaching just below the shoulders of the black zip-front sweater she wore. She wore a wide, black metal-studded belt around her gray skinny jeans, which were shredded at the knees. In addition to the unique choker, she wore long, dangly earrings that sparkled with black and red stones. Her green eyes were lined in black — something neither the Marblehead Junior High dress code nor Chloe's own mother would ever allow. Last week Chloe had managed to get out of the house wearing a thin smear of raspberry-pink lip gloss and it had nearly gotten her sent to the principal's office.

"My name's Chloe."

Taylor offered a confident smile. She didn't look scary, exactly, but she did seem a little goth. Okay, maybe not full-on goth, since her nose and eyebrows weren't pierced, and, as far as Chloe could tell, she wasn't sporting any tattoos, but her style did appear to have major goth potential. *Goth with training wheels,* Chloe thought. *Cool.* Taylor looked to be about twelve, like Chloe was, but Chloe was sure she'd never seen her in school.

"Are you new here?" Chloe asked.

Taylor nodded. "I'm starting school tomorrow."

"That's great. What grade?"

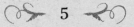

"Seventh."

"I'm in seventh, too."

"Cool."

"Where did you move from?" Chloe asked.

But the girl had turned to gaze at tombstones in the ancient burial ground, and her words overlapped with Chloe's almost as if she were avoiding the question.

"I love old graveyards," she said.

"You do?" Chloe wrinkled her nose. What kind of weirdo *loved* graveyards? She felt herself shudder as it suddenly occurred to her that she was standing on Old Burial Hill breathing normally. If there was any truth to Davis's theory, both Chloe's and Taylor's souls were in serious trouble.

"I like all kinds of historical stuff," Taylor explained. "Antique furniture, historic homes, and especially vintage clothes and jewelry."

"Oh." Chloe smiled, relieved to know that Taylor wasn't some kind of grim gothic ghost-chaser. It also explained the antique choker with its crystal heart charm. "I guess you could call this sweatshirt 'vintage,'" she said, motioning to the ratty old hoodie she had on. "It's from when I was in fifth grade."

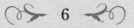

"It's positively ancient!" Taylor laughed.

"But I don't usually wear old clothes," Chloe continued as they fell into step together, leaving the spooky old cemetery behind them. "See, I was going to wear this awesome cardi I got on Main Street but I couldn't find it anywhere this morning. And I had plenty of time to search while I was waiting *forever* to get into the bathroom." She sighed. "It's my favorite sweater and it just, like, *vanished* into thin air."

"Hmmm." Taylor's glitter-polished fingertips went to the crystal at her throat. "Maybe you should look for it . . ." She scowled for a moment, thinking as another autumn breeze lifted the wisps of hair around her face. ". . . at the bottom of your older sister's hamper."

Chloe stopped dead in her tracks. Had she mentioned she had a big sister? She didn't think so. She blinked at Taylor, puzzled. "Um, okay. I'll do that."

"So tell me about Marblehead," Taylor said, the scowl turning to a friendly grin as she changed the subject. "What do kids do for fun around here?"

"Same as anywhere, I guess," Chloe reported. "In the summer we go to the beach a lot. And during the school year it's mostly the movies and the mall." She

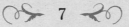

grinned. "If I could, I'd *live* at the mall. Fashion is my passion!"

"Mine too!" said Taylor, indicating her outfit. "Today I look like an escapee from a haunted house, but tomorrow I could go totally preppie. Or hipster. Or whatever strikes my fancy!"

"Awesome," said Chloe. "I tend to stick to whatever's trending at the moment, but I'd love to be more unpredictable!"

"What else are you into?" Taylor asked.

"Music," said Chloe. "Half my allowance goes to clothes and accessories, the other half goes straight to my iPod. Oh, and lately, I've kind of been into drama."

"Drama?" Taylor frowned. "You mean like all those junior high popularity problems and social stress?"

Chloe giggled. "No, not that kind of drama. Although, unfortunately we do have plenty of that at MJHS." She felt a twinge of sadness thinking of the current tension between her and Sam, but she quickly pushed it away. "Drama as in the drama club. You know, the school play."

Taylor's eyes lit up. "There's going to be a school play?"

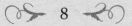

"Yep. I'm gonna audition. Do you like that kind of stuff?"

"I *love* that kind of stuff," Taylor informed her. "Maybe we could try out together?"

"That would be great!" said Chloe, and she meant it. The argument she and Sam had just had was the culmination of two weeks' worth of Chloe begging Sam to join the drama club with her, but Sam could be shy sometimes and the thought of standing up in front of a whole auditorium full of parents, teachers, and students (including Jake Bailey) was way outside her comfort zone.

"Well, I should head home," said Taylor. "Tons of unpacking to do, and if I don't hurry, my older sister is going to take up my whole side of the bedroom closet."

"I feel your pain," said Chloe, imagining that her own big sister, Evie, would surely do the same. "So I'll see you in school tomorrow."

"Yeah, see you there!" Taylor waved and headed off toward the section of Marblehead known as Old Town. It was a charming historic district overlooking the water with homes dating back to the Revolutionary War. Although most of Chloe's friends and classmates lived in the newer houses and

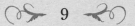

neighborhoods of Marblehead, she'd heard rumors about some of the homes in Old Town being haunted.

As Chloe watched her new friend, Taylor, disappear around a corner, a dark cloud covered the sun.

Despite the warm air, Chloe shivered.

And later, at home, Chloe felt another, even creepier shiver slither up her spine!

But this shiver had nothing to do with the horror of finding her favorite new cardigan with an enormous brownish blotch staining the front of it. This time, Chloe's spine tingled because somehow, inexplicably, Taylor had known exactly where she would find it! After another crazy search of her bedroom, the bathroom, and the laundry room, Chloe had finally discovered the soiled sweater buried at the bottom of her sister Evie's dirty clothes hamper. Just as Taylor predicted!

"Mom!" Chloe stomped down the stairs, shaking the ruined sweater in her fist. "Evie totally destroyed my new yellow cardi! She never even asked if she could borrow it!"

Evie, who was sprawled on the family room sofa

reading a movie magazine, rolled her eyes as Mom hurried in from the kitchen.

"Evie?" asked Mom. "Is this true?"

"I guess," said Evie, flipping a page, completely unconcerned. "But, so what? I mean, she got it on sale. And besides, it's yellow. Nobody wears yellow."

"*You* wore yellow!" Chloe reminded her. "Long enough to spill soy latte on it."

Again, Evie rolled her eyes. "Try vanilla chai tea," she sneered, her face showing her disgust. "Don't you know anything?"

"I know I'm out one brand-new sweater!" Chloe shouted, folding her arms and flopping into a cushy chair.

"Girls, girls!" Mom said in her "just remain calm and no one will get hurt" tone. "Chloe, let me see the sweater. Maybe I can —"

Chloe held up the sweater, cutting her mom off midsentence. It was clear that the hideous brown stain had already seeped deep into the soft yellow wool and dried into the fibers. For life. There was no saving the cardigan and Mom, the laundry guru and pre-soak expert, knew it.

Mom frowned at Evie. "You'll have to replace it," she said firmly. "With your own money."

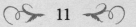

Evie sat up in a huff. "Fine," she said, glaring at Chloe. "I'll replace it. If I *can*. But don't get your hopes up. I'm sure the Everything-Must-Go-Especially-Ugly-Sweaters clearance sale she bought it at is over by now and there aren't any left." She smiled an uppity smile at Chloe. "Where'd you get it, anyway? Seventh Graders R Us?"

Chloe narrowed her eyes. "I got it at that pricey boutique you and all your stuck-up ninth-grade friends shop at all the time!"

The shop was called Envy and it was the coolest store on the quaint little Main Street in town. Chloe had been saving up forever to be able to afford the hip styles they sold there. This had been her first purchase, and now it was ruined. She felt tears prickle behind her eyes. Not only had that sweater fit her perfectly, but the butter color looked great against her fair skin and dark chestnut hair. Samantha had said it even made her blue eyes look bluer.

Samantha. On any other day Chloe would have already been frantically texting her best friend, complaining about how selfish and annoying Evie was, and Samantha would be texting back something sympathetic and funny.

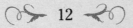

But she couldn't text Sam. She couldn't call her or hop on her bike and pedal the three blocks to Sam's house to complain about Evie in person.

Because for the first time in seven years, Sam and Chloe weren't speaking.

CHAPTER TWO

There were certain things about junior high that you just didn't mess with.

Lunch tables, for example. With very few exceptions, the kids at Marblehead Junior High sat at the same tables, in the same chairs, every day for their entire junior high lives.

Another thing that was cast in stone was the routes to take to class — even if there were several possible ways of getting from, say, gym to history, once you committed to a path you stuck to it.

Most of all, though, the delicate balance of social interaction was absolutely *not* open for debate. Cheerleaders spoke to other cheerleaders, band kids talked to other band kids, math geniuses talked to other math geniuses. Although actually, the genius cliques appeared to be more flexible — it wasn't entirely unheard of to see a computer whiz kid engaged in conversation with a literary scholar *and* a math genius outside the heavy double doors of the MJHS library. Other than that, junior high didn't allow for a lot of social overlap.

That fact of seventh-grade life had never bothered Chloe before. She was perfectly content with her corridor routes, and she loved the fact that every day during Lunch Wave Two she could count on sitting down at the third table on the left, near the window with the bent venetian blind. There she would enjoy her noonday meal with Samantha and their other two best friends, Kimmie Foster and Alyssa Wheaton, and their really good guy friends, Drake and Baxter, who were the only two seventh graders who were good enough to suit up for the school football team.

But on this particular Thursday during Lunch Wave Two, Chloe entered the cafeteria feeling excited and a little bit nervous. That morning in study hall, she had invited her new acquaintance from Old Burial Hill, Taylor, to have lunch with her at the third table on the left.

Technically, she probably should have run the

idea by Sam and the others first, but she and Taylor had been chatting in study hall, planning to swing by the drama club office later in the day to sign up for play tryouts, and the lunch invitation had just slipped out. She had intended to introduce Taylor to Sam in pre-algebra, the one class they all had together, but Sam hadn't so much as made eye contact with Chloe once throughout the entire class period, and she had chickened out.

As Chloe and Taylor made their way through the lunch line, Chloe began to feel uneasy.

"Whoa, what's that?" Taylor asked, motioning toward the pile of beige glop the gray-haired lunch lady had just ladled onto her plate.

"It's a lunchroom specialty," Chloe said, wrinkling her nose. "Tuna noodle casserole. Or as we like to call it, 'tuna noodle casser-rolling on the floor with stomach pain.'" She offered a smile as they reached the sweets section. "But the chocolate cupcakes are fabulous!"

Taylor eyed the available desserts. "I don't see any chocolate cupcakes."

"That's because they're always the first to go," Chloe sighed. "I guess we got here too late." Frowning, she reached for a bowl of jiggly green gelatin that looked older than the lunch lady with the ladle. Taylor settled for a slimy-looking fruit cup.

When they emerged from the kitchen line into the huge lunchroom, Chloe led Taylor directly to her usual table. As they walked, kids turned to get a look at "the new girl." Secretly, Chloe was glad that for her first-day-at-the-new-school outfit, Taylor had wisely veered away from the Goth-lite and hipster sections of her wardrobe, and had instead chosen to wear a very nice pale blue sweater and indigo jeans. Her wavy red hair was pulled half up with a blue barrette and there was none of yesterday's inky black liner rimming her pretty green eyes. She was also wearing her crystal choker.

Samantha, Kimmie, and Alyssa had already seated themselves at their table, and they watched in curious silence as Chloe approached with Taylor in tow. No one looked mad, exactly, but they did look awfully surprised.

"Hi," said Chloe, hoping she sounded more confident than she felt. "Um, this is Taylor. She's new. I met her yesterday and I thought it would be nice if she sat with us instead of eating all alone."

No one could argue with that. And the fact of the matter was that Sam, Kimmie, and Alyssa were among the nicest girls in the class — which, of course, was why Chloe considered them her best friends.

Sam smiled her friendliest smile. "We'd love to have you join us. Grab a seat."

Chloe sent Sam a grateful look as she took her own usual chair and made the introductions.

"You're in my Basic Journalism Writing class, right?" said Alyssa.

"Yeah," said Taylor. "I signed up for that because I wrote for the school newspaper last year and really liked it."

"I signed up for it because it was the only English elective that fit in my schedule," giggled Alyssa. "But so far I don't hate it."

When Taylor was seated, she scanned her lunch tray. "Oops. I forgot to get a drink. "

"C'mon," said Kimmie, standing up and digging into her pocket for change. "I was just going to buy myself a juice at the vending machine. You can do that, or there's free chocolate milk at the end of the lunch line."

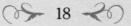

"Thanks," said Taylor.

"I need more salad dressing," Alyssa observed. "I'll walk with you guys."

When the three girls were gone, Chloe turned to Sam. "I'm sorry I was so judgmental about you not wanting to join drama club," she blurted. "It wasn't fair of me, and I feel really bad."

"It's okay," said Sam earnestly. "I was being pouty about it, so I don't blame you for being frustrated. And I'm sorry I was getting all crushy over Jake. You liked him first."

Chloe laughed. "Well, it's not like he knows I'm alive, so there's definitely nothing to apologize for." She poked her fork at the soggy noodles on her plate. "I hate that we've been arguing!"

"I do, too!" Sam reached over and plucked the chocolate cupcake from her lunch tray. "Here," she said, handing the dessert to Chloe. "You're way more chocolate-obsessed than I am. You have it."

"Thanks," said Chloe. Then she launched into the dreadful tale of her ruined yellow sweater. She had just finished telling the story when the three other girls returned.

"That reminds me," said Chloe to Taylor. "How

did you know I'd find my sweater in my sister's laundry? And for that matter, how did you know I have a sister?"

Taylor shook her carton of chocolate milk and gave Chloe a secretive smile. "I just knew."

Chloe frowned. Not the explanation she was hoping for.

"Where are Bax and Drake?" Kimmie asked, scanning the lunchroom.

"Good question," said Chloe. "They should be here by n —" She stopped short, her heart sinking. There, at the fourth table on the right, sat their two best guy friends . . . with the cheerleaders!

"What's up with that?" Alyssa demanded. "Since when do Drake and Baxter talk to cheerleaders?" She lowered her eyebrows. "Especially that snippy Adriana Faulkner!"

"She's such a phony!" Sam observed. "She pretends to be nice, but she talks behind everybody's back."

"Which one's Adriana?" Taylor asked, taking a sip of her chocolate milk.

"The one with the long black hair and the giant ego," Chloe grumbled. Adriana was fawning all over Drake, who was smiling so broadly she was

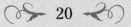

surprised his cheeks didn't burst. Bax just looked as though he couldn't believe his luck. "First seventh grader in history to be voted cheer captain. Drake and Baxter usually sit with us, but I guess they decided they'd rather bask in the dazzling glow of her cheerleaderiness."

"Don't worry," said Taylor, her fingers going to the shimmering crystal heart dangling from her choker, "I'm pretty sure the boys will be back to sitting here tomorrow."

Sam's eyebrows shot up. "How do you know?"

"Well . . ." Taylor gave a little shrug. "Let's just say that they won't be able to sit with Adriana if she's not here, will they?"

"I don't understand," said Alyssa.

Taylor just smiled. Chloe noticed she was still touching her necklace, just like she had the day before on Old Burial Hill. A second later, she'd let go of the crystal and was placing her napkin in her lap.

"So, Taylor," said Sam, changing the subject, "you never told us where you're from. Have you always lived in Massachusetts?"

Taylor nodded, picking up her fork.

"Where in Massachusetts?"

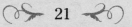

"Oh, not far from here," said Taylor, evasively. "A small town."

"Which small town?" Alyssa asked.

Taylor took a bite of her tuna noodle casserole and grimaced. "This tastes even worse than it looks."

"Here," said Kimmie, handing Taylor the uneaten half of her chicken-salad sandwich. "You can have this. My mom's specialty. Cranberries and walnuts, light on the mayo."

"So . . . which small town?" Chloe asked, repeating Alyssa's question.

Taylor bit into the chicken salad. They all waited as she chewed, then swallowed, then took another sip of milk. "Salem," she said at last. "I'm from Salem, Massachusetts."

Sam's eyes went wide. Kimmie looked a little pale. Alyssa gulped.

"Isn't Salem the town that's famous for —" Chloe began, but Taylor didn't wait for Chloe to finish her question.

"Yes," she said. "Salem is the town that's famous for witches."

*   *   *

After school, Chloe met Sam at her locker.

"Wanna come over after dinner and study for pre-algebra?" Sam asked.

"Definitely!" Chloe frowned, thinking of the big red *F* on the top of her last quiz paper. "I need all the study time I can get." She hesitated. "Should I invite Taylor, too?"

Sam bit her lip. "I don't know . . ."

"Didn't you like her?" Chloe asked. "Kimmie and Alyssa said she seemed cool."

"She did," Sam agreed. "But that whole thing about Bax and Drake not being able to sit with Adriana . . . and that business about knowing where your sweater was." She shrugged. "It was a little . . . unnerving."

"Maybe she's just one of those people with great intuition," Chloe suggested. To be perfectly honest, at first she'd found Taylor's remark about Adriana strange, too, but she decided to give her new friend the benefit of the doubt. Maybe that was just how people acted in Salem.

"Maybe," Sam conceded. "Okay, bring her." She grinned. "Davis will be thrilled. He loves redheads."

The girls giggled. Sam's older brother was in ninth grade and he was totally in girl-crazy mode.

Davis was smart, and funny, and the star of the ninth-grade football team. Secretly, Chloe thought Davis Kendall was even cuter than Jake Bailey, but there was no way she would ever bring herself to admit it to Sam! It would be way too weird.

As Sam closed her locker and slipped into her jean jacket, Taylor came around the corner.

"Hi," she said, her eyes going immediately to the perfectly faded denim of Sam's old jacket. "Wow. Awesome jacket. Is it vintage?"

"Thanks," said Sam. "It was my mom's when she was in high school, so it's really soft and worn in. And I love the way it's frayed at the cuffs and the collar."

"Me too," said Taylor, her voice deepening slightly as her eyes locked on the copper buttons and the faded material. It was a moment before she snapped out of it and turned to Chloe. "Are we still going to sign up for play tryouts together?"

"Sure," said Chloe. She smiled at Sam. "And I'll see you at your house tonight for a pre-algebra cram session."

"You can come, too, if you like," Sam said to Taylor. "Hopefully, you're better at the whole '2x equals y' stuff than Chloe and I are."

When Sam hurried off to catch her bus, Chloe and Taylor headed for the stairwell.

"The drama classroom's on the second floor," said Chloe, feeling giddy that her friends, especially Sam, seemed willing to give Taylor a chance to enter their circle. "That's where the sign-up sheet will be. See, I always take the west stairwell to the second floor. It's out of the way, so almost no one uses it, but I like it because it's never crowded. Most seventh graders use the south stairwell. The east stairwell is the one the eighth and ninth graders use, and I can't stand the way they turn up their noses at seventh graders, like they own the place. The north stairs are strictly for teachers, so that's why I take the west. Anyway, it seems like people are really excited about the play. I heard a bunch of eighth graders are going to audition and —"

"I really like Sam's jean jacket," Taylor interrupted. Her voice was flat and she was staring straight ahead with a blank expression almost as though she hadn't heard a word Chloe had said.

Chloe shrugged. "It's kind of her trademark. Her signature fashion statement. She's not really into clothes and style that much, but it's an accepted fact that she has the coolest jacket in school. Even some

of the popular ninth-grade girls have complimented her on it."

"I want one," said Taylor. Her eyes seemed dulled and her voice icy.

"Well good luck with that," Chloe laughed. "It's probably the only one of its kind. But I guess you could try the thrift stores and vintage shops in town. Maybe the place where you bought your choker?"

Taylor's hand flew to the crystal at her throat so fast that Chloe took a step back. Then Taylor blinked and shook her head, as though shaking off a bad dream. "So, what were you saying about eighth graders?"

"I was saying a lot of them are interested in trying out, so there might be some major competition."

Taylor waggled her eyebrows. "Bring it on!"

The girls giggled.

"I can't wait to find out what play we're doing," said Chloe. "I hope it's a musical. I love to sing." She was hoping for something upbeat, like *Grease* or *Annie*.

"I sing okay," said Taylor. "But I can't dance. When I try, I look like a baby giraffe learning to roller skate."

Picturing that made Chloe laugh.

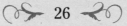

Seconds later, they had arrived at the drama classroom. A gaggle of older girls was huddled around the desk where the sign-up sheet waited. One of them was the eighth-grade queen bee, Jennifer Thomas. It was a generally accepted fact in MJHS that, although Jennifer was your basic mean girl and also an airhead whose grade point average fell some-where between a D-minus and an F, she was the undisputed most popular girl in the school.

Chloe and Taylor waited their turn. When they finally made it to the desk they found a clipboard and a pile of ratty, dog-eared paperback books.

"This must be the script," said Chloe, eagerly snatching a copy from the pile. She frowned at the title. "*The Crucible*, by Arthur Miller," she read aloud. "Never heard of it."

"I have," groaned Taylor plucking her own copy from the pile. "It's about the Salem witch trials. And it's going to call for some pretty intense acting skills."

"That is absolutely correct," came a voice from the back of the classroom.

Chloe turned to see Mr. Wentworth, the ninth-grade English teacher and drama club advisor, standing at the chalkboard. He was a round little gray-haired man in a tweed vest and a bow tie; a pair of wire-framed eyeglasses perched on his nose.

"Hi," said Chloe. "I'm Chloe Rawlings and this is Taylor Dunbar. We're in seventh grade."

"Nice to see the younger students showing an interest in the arts," Mr. Wentworth observed in his crisp British accent. "I think you'll find the subject matter of this production very exciting. *The Crucible* is a sophisticated tale of spite and jealousy set against the historic backdrop of Puritanical New England."

Chloe gave the teacher a weak smile. "Soooo . . . then it's *not* a musical comedy?" she quipped.

"Hardly," replied Mr. Wentworth with a sniff.

"It's a good story," said Taylor. "These snotty girls start accusing people they don't like of being witches and the alleged witches get sent to jail and burned at the stake."

Seriously?

Chloe frowned. "Sounds fascinating."

"Auditions will be tomorrow before homeroom," Mr. Wentworth informed them. With that, he picked up his briefcase and strode out of the room.

As the girls made their way downstairs toward the main lobby, Chloe flipped through the copy

of the play. "Looks like Abigail Williams is the lead character," she noted. "She's the one who starts the big hullabaloo, calling people witches and stuff. Basically, she's a big liar."

"Big liar, big part," said Taylor, her eyes dancing. "It would be great to be cast in that role."

"Yeah," Chloe agreed. Then she mustered her courage and said, "I'm going to read for the role of Abigail."

Unfortunately, she said it at the exact same moment that Taylor piped up with, "I think I'll audition for the part of Abigail."

"Oh," said Chloe.

"Yeah," said Taylor.

They each flashed an awkward smile and continued walking, both of them silent until they reached the main lobby.

"I guess it doesn't really matter what part we want," Chloe said, hoping to sound more cheerful than she felt. "I'm sure the lead will go to Jennifer Thomas."

A slant of sunlight through the glass doors of the lobby reflected off Taylor's crystal choker and flashed in Chloe's eyes.

"Who's Jennifer Thomas?" Taylor demanded.

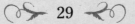

"She's that really pretty blond eighth grader we saw by the sign-up sheet," said Chloe, "and she's always picked for everything. Well, except for once she went to New York City and auditioned for a commercial for pimple cream, but she didn't get the job."

"'Cause she didn't have any acting skills?"

"'Cause she didn't have any pimples." Chloe sighed and opened the door that led to the front steps. "Well, I guess I'll see you at Sam's tonight," she said.

"Yeah, about that," said Taylor. "I was thinking since the auditions are tomorrow, maybe we should work on our lines."

Chloe considered it. The audition was first thing in the morning, which barely even gave them time to memorize the scene, let alone perfect the character. Despite the fact that Jennifer Thomas seemed like a shoo-in for the lead, Chloe didn't see any point in not giving it her best effort. She knew Sam would understand. There'd be time to study math over the weekend, and Sam knew how much being in the play meant to her.

"You're right," said Chloe. "I'll text Sam and explain that we won't be there."

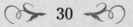

"No, let me," offered Taylor, taking out her cell. "Besides, I need to put Sam's number into my phone, so this is a good opportunity."

"Okay, just tell her we're sorry and we'll take a rain check."

Chloe rattled off Sam's digits and Taylor punched them into her phone, saving the number to her contacts. Then she typed in the message and hit SEND.

"Done," said Taylor. "See you tomorrow, Chloe."

"See you, Taylor."

Chloe practically sprinted home. She couldn't wait to start preparing her lines.

CHAPTER THREE

The next morning, Chloe's dad dropped her off at school early. She was practically bouncing up and down in her seat with nervous excitement. Last night, she'd approached her rehearsal like a seasoned theater professional, using the Internet to study up on the play. She read about the themes, the characters, and the historical significance of what was considered a very important play. After much consideration, Chloe decided that her interpretation of Abigail would be an understated one; she'd play the part of the jealous girl with a quiet, calculating air, allowing the character's evil nature to sizzle beneath the surface . . . like lava in a volcano.

After hours of reciting her lines in front of her bedroom mirror, Chloe did her audition scene for her family. Of course Mom and Dad said she gave a fabulous performance, but to her shock, even Evie had said she was good! To be precise, Evie commented that Chloe's dramatic choice to play the role with a "subtle, simmering fury" was very effective. Chloe figured that "subtle, simmering fury" was a phrase Evie had come across while reading some five-star film review in one of her movie magazines. Chloe didn't care where Evie had gotten the lingo. A compliment was a compliment.

"Break a leg," said Dad, as Chloe bolted across the parking lot.

She hurried into school, which was eerily empty at this time of the morning. The first-floor corridors were dim; she could see a few teachers here and there, behind the closed doors of their classrooms, getting a jump on the day's lesson plans.

Out of habit, Chloe made her way to the west stairwell. It was a good thing she knew the route, because she was barely paying attention as she went over her lines in her head. When she reached the stairwell, she saw that the windowless space was dark. Clasping the handrail, Chloe began to climb the stairs, but in her mind she was imagining herself as the character of Abigail Williams.

"I never knew what pretense Salem was, I never knew the lying lessons I was taught," she whispered, reciting the lines she had memorized into the shadowy stairwell. She had only climbed three steps, but the powerful words echoed upward into the cavernous space.

Chloe was so into her last-minute rehearsing that it was a split second before she registered what was happening: She felt something slam into her shoulder and tug. And in the next heartbeat, Chloe was toppling backward.

Instinctively, she twisted her body around so that her hands, and not the back of her skull, would collide with the rough cement floor. She hit hard; lightning bolts of pain shot up from her wrists and kneecaps. She vaguely thought she heard something — or someone — scurry toward the exit; a pale shaft of light from the corridor lit the stairwell when the door opened. With great effort Chloe lifted her head to see who had attacked her, but the door had already swung closed, and all she could hear was the muffled sound of the culprit's footsteps escaping down the long interior corridor.

Feeling dazed and afraid, Chloe managed to stand. The palms of her hands stung and her knees

were throbbing. But the pain was nothing compared to the realization that someone had purposely yanked her down the stairs! It didn't make sense. Who would want to hurt her? She didn't have any enemies.

Shaken and fighting back tears, Chloe took hold of the handrail and made her way to the second floor.

The drama classroom was packed with theatrical hopefuls. Jennifer Thomas was there, of course, with her clique of snooty BFFs to cheer her on.

Taylor was sitting quietly in a far corner of the room. She waved, and Chloe limped over to sit with her.

"Are you okay?" asked Taylor. "You're walking funny."

"Something crazy just happened," Chloe whispered in a shaky voice. "I think someone tried to push me down the stairs!"

Taylor's eyes went wide with concern. "That's terrible!" Taylor patted Chloe's shoulder. "But what do you mean you 'think' someone did it?"

"Well, it was kind of dark in the stairwell, and I

wasn't really paying attention." She glanced toward the front of the room, where Mr. Wentworth was shuffling through some papers. "I should probably tell a teacher."

Taylor bit her lip. "I guess you could, but what would you say exactly? That you fell down the stairs, but you're not sure why? And that maybe there's a possibility that someone attacked you, but you don't know for certain?"

Chloe frowned. That sounded ridiculous. She was pretty sure she'd been pushed, but then again, it could have been an accident — maybe some other student was rushing and just bumped into her by mistake. Chloe had been awfully engrossed in reciting her lines. Maybe she'd misread the whole incident. And if she mentioned to Mr. Wentworth that she only suspected she'd been pushed, maybe he'd think she was too flaky to cast in the play.

"I guess you're right." Chloe massaged her aching knees. "And besides, it could have been worse. I was only three steps up at the time." She forced a chuckle. "My dad did tell me to break a leg, but I don't think he meant it literally."

Taylor gave her a sympathetic smile. "Well, you

sure look great!" she said, eyeing Chloe's outfit and hair.

"You think?" Chloe's hand went nervously to one of her braids. "I know the sign-up sheet didn't say anything about wardrobe, but I figured it couldn't hurt."

That morning as Chloe was getting dressed, she'd been inspired to search the Internet for pictures of colonial fashions and hairstyles. By doing her hair in two long braids — or plaits, as they were called in the seventeenth century — and wearing a frumpy little calico blouse she'd found in the back of her closet, she'd managed to pull together a look that had her feeling exactly like a girl from puritanical New England! Of course, she'd stuffed a sweater in her backpack to change into later; she certainly didn't want to go through an entire day of junior high looking like she should be spinning yarn and churning butter.

Taylor, who, in addition to her crystal necklace, was wearing a perfectly modern lilac cami under a little ruffle-trimmed bolero and a pair of bright purple cords, ran a hand through her mass of auburn waves. "I wish I'd thought of dressing for the part," she mumbled, her fingers trailing from her curls to the choker at her neck. Her mouth quirked into a frown. "You'll have an unfair advantage now."

The comment seemed a little snarky to Chloe. "I didn't do it to be unfair," she said defensively. "I did it to get into character."

Taylor rolled her eyes, giving the choker a little tug. "Whatever."

Then Mr. Wentworth was clapping his hands for attention and auditions were underway.

Jennifer Thomas went first. She hadn't memorized all the lines, but since she wasn't exactly known for being a brainiac, Mr. Wentworth said she could read her lines from the book. Except for the fact that she punctuated every line with a toss of her long, sun-streaked blond hair, Jennifer gave a respectable performance.

"Does she think she's auditioning for a shampoo commercial?" Taylor whispered, and Chloe had to bite her lip to keep from laughing.

When Jennifer finished, her friends applauded like crazy, and Jennifer beamed, flipping her hair all over the place.

Mr. Wentworth didn't comment, just made some notes on a pad and said, "Next . . ."

Billy Tibbs, a ninth-grade boy with braces, read for the lead male role of John Proctor, and a shy eighth-grade girl named Madison Arnold read for the part of his wife, Elizabeth. Mr. Wentworth's expression gave no clue as to what he thought of either performance. Again, he just scribbled on his pad and barked, "Next."

It was Taylor's turn. She walked confidently to the front of the room and took her place. Chloe hated to admit it, but she was torn between hoping her new friend did an awesome job, and fearing that she'd be so good that Chloe herself wouldn't stand a chance.

"You may begin," said Mr. Wentworth.

Taylor was quite good. She interpreted the part of the young, envious, and cruel Abigail Williams with a booming voice and exaggerated facial expressions. Her read had great energy and no small amount of anger. Chloe kept sneaking glances at Wentworth, trying to determine what he thought of Taylor's audition, but his face remained blank.

When Taylor was done, Chloe clapped as hard as she could. This prompted Jennifer's friends to shoot her some icy looks.

"Next," said Mr. Wentworth.

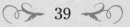

It was Chloe's turn to make her way to the front of the room. She swallowed hard, her eyes darting nervously from Jennifer and her little group, to Wentworth, to Taylor.

Taylor's face was still flushed from her enthusiastic read, but what really surprised Chloe was that instead of flashing a smile of encouragement, Taylor's expression was almost as cold and competitive as the look on Jennifer's face.

Finally, Mr. Wentworth looked up from his notes to focus on Chloe. To her utter shock, a hint of a grin — his first of the morning — appeared on his face.

"The plaits are a very nice touch, Miss Rawlings."

"Um, thanks," gulped Chloe, careful not to meet Taylor's eyes.

"You may begin."

Chloe took a deep breath, allowing the character of Abigail Williams to take over. As she had expected, the other Abigail wannabes had raised their voices, shouting and stomping around in standard villainess form. But Chloe was going to stick to her decision to play the role with a subtle edge. She narrowed her eyes, and, keeping her voice low but smoldering with fury, she recited the powerful words. *"If anyone breathe a word or the edge of a*

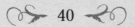

word about the other things, I will come to you in the black of some terrible night, and I will bring with me a pointy reckoning that will shudder you! And you know I can do it!"

As she uttered those final words into the silence, Chloe flung one arm outward to point a trembling finger at her invisible enemy; her face was carved into an expression of utter rage.

No one moved. No one spoke. The closing line seemed to shimmer in the stillness. Chloe held her pose dramatically, letting her eyes scan the room.

Taylor's mouth had dropped open.

Billy and Madison looked on in awe.

Even Jennifer Thomas seemed impressed.

And Mr. Wentworth . . .

. . . smiled!

"Nicely done, Chloe Rawlings," he murmured, circling something on his notepad. "Nicely done."

By the time everyone had finished auditioning, there were only five minutes to spare before the homeroom bell. As Chloe and Taylor made their way out of the drama classroom, they found themselves right behind Jennifer and company.

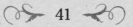

"You were, like, *so* incredible, Jen!" chirped one of her minions.

"Totally!" agreed another. "Way to emote!"

Jennifer didn't thank them. She didn't have to. This was their job and they knew it. "I forgot a line," she muttered.

"So what?" piped a third girl. "Your *hair* looked amazing!"

"Well, I *know* that!" said Jennifer tossing her blond locks. "It always looks amazing." She sighed, pulling an elastic band out of her bling-encrusted backpack to gather her hair up into a high ponytail. Unfortunately, she inadvertently whipped Taylor in the face with her hair while she was at it.

"Hey!"

Jennifer whirled, leveling Taylor with a look. "Problem, seventh grader?" she sneered, winding the hair tie around her sleekly perfect pony.

"You think you're so cool because you're blond!" huffed Taylor.

"No," said Jennifer, "I think I'm so cool because I *am* so cool. The blond thing is just a bonus!"

"I could be blond, too, if I wanted," said Taylor, with a snort. "Can you say *hydrogen peroxide*?"

It occurred to Chloe that, actually, maybe Jennifer couldn't.

"Are you suggesting that Jennifer dyes her hair?" one of the minions gasped.

"No!" croaked Chloe. "She's not suggesting that at all!"

"She'd better not be!" hissed Jennifer. "Because my hair color is completely natural! I mean, duh! Dyed hair doesn't shine like this! And not that it's any of your business, seventh grader, but my hairdresser says I happen to have very fragile follicles. So I wouldn't put chemicals in my hair if my life depended on it!"

With that, Jennifer swung her gem-studded backpack onto her shoulder. "Come on, girls. I have gym first period. And all I can say is those grungy locker room showers better have hot water today. Last week it was only lukewarm!"

"Did you mention it to the custodian?" asked Minion Number One, as the group set off down the hall.

"Well," said Jennifer, "if by 'mention it' you mean, did I threaten his life if he didn't fix it? Then yes, I did."

The girls laughed, disappearing around the corner at the far end of the hall.

When they were gone, Taylor folded her arms. "Fragile follicles! Why does she get to have such gorgeous, silky blond hair when I'm stuck with these dumb red-brown snarls? Where's the justice? Her hair looks like sunshine; my hair looks like rusted springs!"

"That's not true," Chloe assured her. "Your hair is pretty! It's unique."

"Unique is just another way of saying ugly."

"No it isn't!"

"Well then it's just another way of saying 'not blond.'" Taylor sighed bitterly. "It's not *fair* that she gets good hair and I don't."

Chloe could only stare at her friend. She'd never heard anyone sound so jealous — not to mention ridiculous — before. Since when did hair color have anything to do with fair play? If she remembered her science notes correctly, it had to do with heredity and DNA; the concept of justice didn't enter into it at all.

"I happen to know that some people think red hair is way more attractive than blond," Chloe said as she started off down the hallway. There were only three minutes left before the first bell, and the seventh-grade homerooms were all the way on the opposite side of the building, down on the first floor. Chloe still had to duck into the girls' lav and change out of her pseudo-colonial attire.

"Who?" snapped Taylor, scampering to catch up to her. "Who thinks that?"

"Um, well, Davis Kendall for one." Just saying Davis's name brought a little blush to Chloe's cheeks. "He's Samantha's older brother, and he's one of the cutest boys in the whole ninth grade. According to Sam, Davis totally digs redheads."

This information seemed to calm Taylor's anger a bit.

"Can you keep a secret?" Chloe asked.

Taylor nodded.

"Well, I kind of have a crush on Davis. I mean, he'd never like me back or anything 'cause I'm only in seventh and I'm his sister's best friend. But if I could pick any boy in the whole school to like me, it would totally be Davis."

Taylor giggled. "I swear I won't tell anyone," she promised.

They walked on until they reached the hallway that led to the science wing, which housed the planetarium and the lab classrooms.

"I've got to go," Taylor said abruptly. "I'll see you at lunch."

"Oh . . ." Chloe blinked "Okay."

She watched as Taylor spun on her heel and took off down the science corridor. With only two minutes remaining, Chloe would have to double her pace to avoid being late for homeroom.

With a shudder, she decided that this time she'd take the south stairwell.

CHAPTER FOUR

Chloe's stop in the girls' bathroom to change her shirt had taken longer than she'd expected, and she'd wound up skidding into her homeroom classroom two and a half minutes after the bell.

"Tardy!" Mrs. Winkle, her homeroom teacher, pronounced, marking the offense in the roll book with her red pen.

"Sorry," mumbled Chloe, taking her seat. Then Mrs. Winkle shushed them for the morning announcements, and Chloe sank happily into her own thoughts.

She'd rocked her audition, no question about it! Not to be conceited, but her reading had been way better than Jennifer's and Taylor's. Chloe had also out-acted the ninth grader who'd peer-tutored Sam for her last French test and three other eighth graders, including Caroline Fletcher, who was said to be a cello prodigy and the best player on the girls' travel soccer team. Bottom line: If Mr. Wentworth didn't give Chloe the part of Abigail Williams it was either because he was completely incompetent or because Jennifer Thomas had threatened *his* life along with the custodian's.

After homeroom, Chloe headed directly for Sam's locker. Since Chloe's first-period English class was only two doors down from Sam's locker, this was their standard morning routine. Baxter usually joined them there, too. His locker was right next to Sam's.

"Hi, Sam!"

Sam shoved a book into her locker. "Hi."

"Auditions went really well, I think," Chloe rambled on, leaning up against Baxter's locker door. "I remembered all my lines, and I think I was really feeling the character."

"Good for you," Sam grumbled.

Chloe frowned. "Is something wrong?"

"Maybe." Sam slammed her locker closed, causing Chloe to jump. This was not like Samantha at all.

Chloe was truly confused. "Are you mad at me?" she asked, but she realized that Sam didn't look mad so much as hurt.

"Way to totally blow me off last night," said Sam in a tight voice. "I made a pre-algebra-appropriate playlist on my iPod to study by. I prepared a study guide, and I put out study snacks and everything!" She sounded as if she were trying not to cry. "And then you didn't show up. You didn't even call to say you couldn't make it!"

Chloe blinked, stunned by the accusation. "I did so call! Well, technically, I texted." She shook her head because, strictly speaking, that wasn't true either. "Taylor texted, actually."

"No she didn't."

"Yes she did!" Chloe insisted. "I saw her. I even told her what to say in the text."

"Oh?" Sam gave her a challenging look. "And what was that exactly?"

"I told her to tell you that we were sorry, but we had to work on our lines because the audition was this morning. I told her to tell you we'd do it another time."

We?" Sam opened her locker again to grab her vocab workbook. "So I was cramming for pre-algebra

all alone, while you and Taylor were working on your lines together?" Sam looked even more hurt than she had before.

"No!" Chloe said quickly. "I was at my house, and she was at hers. We didn't practice together!"

"You didn't?"

"No!" Chloe wasn't sure why this particular point was an issue, but clearly it mattered to Sam so she repeated it: "We didn't rehearse together at all."

This seemed to soothe Sam a little.

Encouraged, Chloe tugged her phone out of the pocket of her jeans. "I'll ask Taylor about the text right now."

Sam waited patiently while Chloe thumbed in the message to Taylor. The response was practically immediate:

OMG! Must have entered Sam's # wrong!

Can I make it up 2 U guys with a sleepover at my house 2nite?

Junk food & party games! K. and A. are invited 2.

Chloe showed the message to Sam. "See? It was all just a mistake."

Sam shrugged. "I suppose." She didn't look as completely convinced as Chloe would have liked, but it was better than nothing.

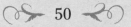

"So are we okay?" Chloe asked.

"Yeah, we're okay." Sam gave her a sheepish look. "I guess I just felt bad because I thought . . ."

"Thought what?"

Sam lowered her eyes, embarrassed. "I thought maybe you would rather start hanging out with Taylor instead of me."

"Are you kidding?" Automatically, Chloe threw her arms around Sam and hugged her tight. "You're my best friend. No way is that gonna happen! Ever!"

"What's not gonna happen ever?" Baxter asked, appearing beside them and banging open his locker.

"Nothing," said Sam, smiling at Chloe.

Suddenly, Chloe remembered what happened yesterday in the cafeteria. "Long time no see, Bax," she said coolly. "Or more like long time no lunch."

"Huh?" Baxter took off his baseball cap and stuffed it into his locker. "What are you talking about?"

"You didn't sit with us in the lunchroom yesterday," Sam reminded him. "It looked like you had a better offer."

Baxter looked thoughtful. "Adriana, you mean?"

"And the entire rest of the pep squad," said Chloe.

"Yeah." Bax rolled his eyes. "Cheerleaders are like pudding cups. They come in a pack."

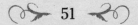

"Maybe so," said Sam. "But that doesn't explain why you sat with them instead of us."

"Yeah, *us*," Chloe echoed. "Your *friends*!"

"It was Drake's idea," said Baxter. "He's got a thing for Adriana."

"Him and about six zillion other boys," Sam pointed out.

"True," said Baxter. "But six zillion other boys don't have fathers who are president of the Athletic Booster Club."

Chloe frowned. What the heck was an athletic booster? A high chair for short athletes?

"See, it's like this," Bax continued. "Drake's dad heads up the parents' organization that raises extra money for the sports teams and helps decide how the athletic department budget gets spent."

"What's that got to do with Adriana?" Sam wondered.

"She's cheer captain. And she wants the Booster Club to spend the money they raised for the JV archery team on new uniforms for the cheerleaders instead."

Chloe crunched an eyebrow at Bax. "We *have* a JV archery team?"

"No," said Bax. "Which is why the Boosters raised the money. To start one."

Sam rolled her eyes. "And sneaky Adriana thought that if she flirted with Drake, she could con him into talking his dad *out* of spending the money on bows and arrows and *into* dropping a bundle on new cheer skirts instead."

"Exactly," said Baxter, closing his locker. "Drake's not gonna do it, of course. He just kind of liked the idea of letting Miss Big Deal Adriana suck up to him for a while."

Boys, thought Chloe. "So we'll see you at lunch today, then?"

Baxter nodded. "An archery team! Can you believe that? The thought of it just makes me *quiver*." With that, he burst into hysterical laughter.

"I don't get it," said Chloe.

"Quiver!" said Baxter. "You know — that thing archery dudes wear on their backs to hold their arrows! Haven't you ever seen a Robin Hood flick?"

"Archery dudes are called archers," Sam corrected, giggling. "But that was a good one, Bax." Sam's cheeks turned a little pink. "And by the way, good luck in the football game tomorrow."

"Thanks, Sammy!"

Then Baxter surprised Chloe by snapping Samantha a wink before galloping off down the hall.

She was about to comment on that flirtatious little gesture when her phone chimed, alerting her that she'd just received a new text message. She read it, and felt her stomach drop to her feet.

"What is it?" Sam asked.

In reply, Chloe showed her the text. It was from Kimmie, who just happened to be in the same homeroom as a certain seventh-grade cheer captain. The message was short and to the point:

Adriana = ABSENT!! :0

When Chloe took her seat at the lunch table, Sam, Kimmie, and Alyssa were already there. She noticed that Kimmie looked pale; she hadn't even touched her food, which was unusual for her. Kimmie was the tiniest of the four of them but she had the biggest appetite. Clearly, the fact that Taylor had "predicted" that Adriana wouldn't be in school today had Kimmie pretty spooked.

Truthfully, Chloe had been a little freaked out herself at first, but now that she'd had the whole morning to think it over, she'd decided it had to be just a creepy coincidence.

"It's scary!" Kimmie whispered. "Adriana's, like, *never* absent."

"That's probably because she can't stand the thought of not being the center of attention for even one day," Chloe joked.

"It's not funny, Chloe!" Alyssa shook her head. "It was like Taylor did something to *cause* Adriana to be out of school."

Chloe rolled her eyes. "C'mon, Lyss. Taylor's not like that."

"I know you like her," said Sam reasonably, "and I understand why you're sticking up for her. But you've got to admit, Chloe, it's strange."

"She was fiddling with that weird necklace of hers," Kimmie recalled. "Maybe the crystal has powers!"

Chloe couldn't believe what she was hearing. "Seriously?"

Kimmie shrugged and poked at the macaroni and cheese on her plate. "It's possible. I mean, she is from Salem. Maybe her crystal got some of that old-time Salem magic stuck to it before Taylor moved. Maybe Taylor can't help what happens when she wears it."

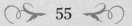

"That's ridiculous!" Chloe shook her head in disbelief. "Guys, really. Halloween is over."

They sat quietly for a moment.

"I agree with Chloe," said Sam at last. "It's silly to think Taylor's crystal has powers, or that she did anything to Adriana."

"So does this mean we're going to her sleepover?" Kimmie asked, her voice a nervous squeak.

"Of course we are," said Chloe. "It'll be fun."

Kimmie and Alyssa exchanged looks.

"Fine," said Alyssa. "I'll go. But only because I don't want her zapping me with that crystal choker!" She sighed, biting into a carrot stick. "There's an old saying about diamonds being a girl's best friend; I just hope it doesn't turn out that crystals are a girl's worst enemy!"

Chloe laughed, but something told her Alyssa wasn't trying to be funny.

CHAPTER FIVE

Chloe was really excited about Taylor's slumber party. Despite everything Kimmie, Alyssa, and Sam had said at lunch, Chloe believed that Taylor was a cool person and she hoped the sleepover would allow her friends to see that, too.

So she and Sam had met at Sam's house after school to bake a batch of gooey caramel-pecan brownies for the party. Kimmie's mom was going to send a huge container of her famous oatmeal-butterscotch cookies. Alyssa promised to bring four super-sized bags of snacks: potato chips, cheese puffs, nacho chips, and honey-mustard pretzel bites, and Taylor would provide not only the pizza but every possible variety of soda as well.

Taylor's house was one of the most charming historic homes in Old Town. Among other cool features like narrow hidden stairways and gleaming wide-plank floors, the house boasted a fireplace in every room, including the bedroom Taylor shared with her big sister, Jenna. Luckily, Jenna was babysitting across the street, so the girls had the room to themselves for the time being. Chloe especially liked the fact that the window above Taylor's bed provided a gorgeous view of the ocean. A plump moon was already casting a glistening white pathway across the water while the girls ate supper.

"This is gonna be the best sleepover ever!" Chloe declared.

Kimmie nodded her agreement and chomped into another slice of double-cheese and pepperoni.

The warm spell they'd been experiencing had ended that afternoon; temperatures had plummeted, and the night outside was frosty. As soon as they finished dinner, the girls bundled up in their snuggliest pj's, fuzziest slippers, and plushest bathrobes. Taylor's dad lit a fire in the fireplace in Taylor's room to offset the chill, and the girls arranged their sleeping bags around the safety screen. Golden firelight

flickered, casting a cozy amber light into the room. Chloe couldn't help but notice that the far corners of the bedroom were bathed in shadow, but she was determined not to let that bother her as she flopped down on her bedroll.

"Let's play a game!" she suggested.

"Truth or dare!" Kimmie and Alyssa chorused.

"Classic slumber party game!" said Taylor, giggling. "Okay, I'll go first." She turned to Chloe, smiling. "Truth or dare?"

"Truth," said Chloe.

"Okay." Taylor's hand rested on the crystal choker and suddenly her tone became deadly serious. "Truthfully, of all the people in this room, who do you consider your closest friend?"

Chloe blinked. "Huh?"

"Out of the four of us," Taylor clarified, "who do you like most?"

What a loaded question! Why would Taylor put her on the spot like that? The truth of course was that Sam was Chloe's best friend; she had been since first grade. But to say it out loud, in front of Kimmie and Alyssa and even Taylor, would be just plain rude.

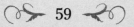

Is it too late to switch to dare? Chloe wondered.

"Well?" Taylor prompted, her eyes flashing in the fiery glow. "You have to answer. Those are the rules."

Even though it was freezing outside, the blazing fire — and the horrible question — were making Chloe sweat. "Phew, that fireplace throws off major heat!" she said. Stalling for time, she pretended to be occupied with pushing up the sleeves of her fleece pajamas.

"Now that you mention it, it is kinda warm in here," Taylor agreed. She stood up to unwrap her thick chenille robe, and as she did, the clasp of her choker snagged on the loopy material. As Taylor tugged off the bathrobe, the choker dropped from her neck, landing with a jangle on top of her sleeping bag.

"Oops!" She bent to pick up the necklace, which she tossed into the closet. "Okay, back to the game. Where were we?"

"You just asked Chloe who her best friend is," Alyssa reminded her.

Taylor frowned. "I did?"

The four other girls nodded.

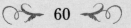

"Well, you don't have to answer," Taylor said apologetically. "I'm sure I was just goofing around when I asked. It's a dumb question. I totally take it back!"

This seemed peculiar, but as far as Chloe could tell Taylor was being completely sincere. She let out a deep sigh of relief.

"Somebody else go," Taylor suggested.

"I will," said Kimmie, turning to Alyssa. "Lyss, truth or dare?"

"Dare!" Alyssa grinned. "And make it a good one!"

"Okay! I dare you to go, all by yourself, down those spooky old back stairs that lead to the dark, empty kitchen, and . . ."

Alyssa gulped. "And?"

"And . . ." Kimmie's face broke into a huge smile, "bring me the rest of the pepperoni pizza!"

"Oh, man!" said Alyssa. "I thought you were gonna make me do something terrifying!"

"That *is* terrifying," Chloe noted. "For Kimmie's stomach! She already ate five slices of pizza, half a bag of nacho chips, three brownies, and a cookie."

Kimmie grinned and fluttered her eyelashes. "Can I help it if I have an extra-fast metabolism?"

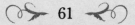

Alyssa squirmed out of her sleeping bag and set out on her mission. Two minutes later she'd returned with not only Kimmie's pizza, but also the nacho chips and cheese puffs, a bottle of grape soda, and the remaining brownies.

"My turn," said Sam. With a determined expression, she turned to Taylor. "Truth or dare."

"Truth!"

Sam looked as if she'd been hoping Taylor would pick that option. "All right," she said in a frank tone, "be honest. How did you know that Chloe would find her yellow cardigan in Evie's laundry? And what happened to Adriana Faulker that kept her out of school today?"

Chloe's eyes went wide. Alyssa let out a tiny gasp. Even Kimmie froze, pizza slice hovering in midair halfway to her mouth. They couldn't believe Sam had just asked those questions. But they were all glad she had.

"Don't forget," said Sam with a solemn nod. "The name of the game is *truth* or dare."

For a moment, Taylor said nothing, looking from one curious face to the next. After what seemed like forever she shook her head. "I seriously have no idea what you're talking about."

"Just tell us," said Chloe. "We promise we won't be upset!"

"Tell you *what*?" Taylor turned up her hands, her brow knit in confusion.

"If your choker has powers!" Kimmie blurted.

"Yeah," Alyssa chimed in. "Is it . . . magical? Enchanted? Or radioactive? Just spill it. What's the deal?"

"Magical?" Now Taylor's eyebrows shot upward in surprise. "Enchanted?"

Actually, a much darker word was floating around in Chloe's mind: *cursed*. But she couldn't bring herself to say it.

"Well you were fiddling with your choker when you told us Adriana wouldn't be in school," Sam pointed out. "We thought maybe the crystal thingy was some kind of magic charm!"

"With some wicked life of its own that no mortal being could control," Alyssa added.

Chloe sighed. "That's a little dramatic, Lyss, dontcha think?"

Taylor was shaking her head in amazement. "A magic charm?" she giggled. "Oh, please!" The next thing the girls knew, Taylor was literally rolling on the floor laughing. She laughed so hard that tears began to roll down her cheeks. Her sleepover guests could only gape at her.

Several minutes passed before she'd settled down enough to catch her breath. "I guess I could see where you might think that," she conceded. "I was the one who mentioned the whole Salem witch connection. But cross my heart and hope to die, guys, I'm pretty sure my choker has no magic powers, since it's just a funky piece of vintage costume jewelry I bought in an antique shop."

"But what about my sweater?" asked Chloe.

"That," said Taylor, "is what you call an educated guess. See, my first clue was that a piece of clothing had gone missing and my second was that you'd just told me you had to wait forever to get into the bathroom. I know from personal experience that not only are older sisters the biggest bathroom hogs on the planet, they also have a tendency to borrow things from their younger sisters without permission. Jenna borrowed my favorite capri pants three years ago, and I haven't seen them since."

Chloe let out a long rush of breath. "No wonder you knew where my sweater would be."

"That still doesn't explain what happened to Adriana," said Sam.

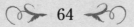

"Oh, that!" Taylor gave a dismissive wave of her hand. "When I went back to the lunch line to get my milk, Adriana was there. She had just gotten a text from her mother."

"You read her text message?" asked Alyssa.

"Of course not. She read it out loud to one of her cheerleader friends. Her mom was texting to remind her to tell her homeroom teacher she'd be absent Friday because they had some big important family thing out of town." Taylor looked hurt. "Even if I had a magic charm, do you really think I'd use it to hurt Adriana, or anyone else for that matter?"

Guilty looks passed between the four girls.

"I guess we were kind of afraid you might," Chloe confessed. "I mean, we haven't known you very long, and it was a pretty wild coincidence."

"True," said Taylor. "Well, I hope you believe me when I say that I would never do anything like that."

"We do now!" Kimmie assured her, popping a piece of pepperoni into her mouth.

"Okay, then," said Taylor. "Enough of this truth or dare stuff. Let's do something really interesting!"

"Like what?" said Sam.

Taylor smiled. "Ghost stories!"

 65

The flames hissed and crackled in the fireplace, casting dancing shadows on the walls of Taylor's bedroom. The only other light was the cold, milky glow of the moon filtering through the lace curtains.

"The year was 1692!" said Taylor. "And Salem, Massachusetts was a dangerous place to be. The pious townspeople lived in fear, for stories abounded of wicked ones among them who went into the woods at midnight. Midnight! The hour when spirits roam the earth and all manner of evil is possible!"

"Wow," Sam whispered out of the corner of her mouth to Chloe. "She's good at this."

Chloe nodded, her eyes going to the clock on the nightstand. It was eight minutes to twelve, which was not exactly comforting considering what Taylor had just said about roaming spirits. She pulled her sleeping bag up around her shoulders and slid closer to Sam.

"Why would anyone go into the woods at midnight?" Alyssa asked.

"Why else?" Taylor's answer was a snakelike hiss: "To conjure evil and cast spells!"

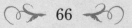

Kimmie gave a yelp of terror and stuffed a brownie into her mouth as Taylor continued.

"In Salem there lived a woman called Martha. She was a brown-eyed beauty, and very vain. She dressed in gowns made from only the most expensive cloth, and she even wore jewelry, which the Colonial New Englanders strongly frowned upon. Worst of all, she was known to have evil spirits as her most loyal cohorts."

"What's a cohort?" asked Kimmie.

"A friend," answered Sam.

Kimmie frowned. "Then why didn't she just say *friend*?"

"Because *cohort* sounds better."

"Not to me, it doesn't."

"It's more authentic," said Chloe.

"Oh. Um, what's *authentic*?"

"It means 'old school.'"

"Got it." Kimmie grabbed a handful of cheese puffs and nodded at Taylor. "Keep going."

"It was a fact known throughout the town that Martha was in love with a man named Zachary . . ."

"Wait. Witches can fall in love?"

"Apparently."

"*Shhhh.* Let her tell the story!"

"Sorry. Go on, please."

"Thank you." Taylor shifted closer to the fireplace; now the flames only lit her face from one side, leaving the other half in darkness, as though she were two halves of the same person.

Creepy! Chloe pulled the sleeping bag tighter and shivered.

"Zachary was a good man, and he had no plan to marry a wicked witch. But Martha refused to accept that. She made it known to all that if she could not have Zachary for her own then no other woman would. Ever! And if she had to use black magic to see to it, she would!"

Chloe smiled. "Sounds like ol' Martha was the jealous type."

Samantha giggled. "Ya think?"

"One day a woman named Arabella arrived in Salem. She had come from across the sea to live in the new world and make a life for herself in the commonwealth of Massachusetts."

"So she was the new girl in town," Alyssa mused. "Like you!"

"Arabella was more beautiful than any woman in Salem, even Martha. But unlike Martha, she was good and kind and friendly, and it wasn't long before all the townsfolk came to adore her. Especially . . ."

Taylor paused, glancing around at the girls.

"Zachary?" Chloe guessed.

"Yes!" Taylor nodded. "Within a fortnight —"

"What's a fortnight?" Kimmie asked.

"Two weeks. *Shhhh!*"

"Within a fortnight, Zachary professed his love for Arabella, and asked for her hand in marriage."

"Awww," sighed Alyssa, munching on a nacho chip. "That's sweet."

"It was," Taylor agreed. "Way romantic. And all of Salem was pleased with the match."

Now Chloe felt a chill as the half of Taylor's face that was lit by the fire went grim.

"But there was someone who did not share in their joy. Can you guess who?"

"Martha!" cried Kimme, Alyssa, and Sam.

"Martha!" Taylor moaned the name in a deep voice.

To Chloe's relief, Taylor shifted again so that her face was fully lit; she looked whole again.

"What did Martha do?" Sam asked anxiously.

"She was positively consumed with jealousy!" cried Sam. "Whenever she saw Zachary walking with Arabella, Martha would seethe with envy. She would become so enraged that her once-beautiful face would turn fiery red and squish up, contorting into a hideous mask of hatred! Legend has it that her jealousy was so powerful that her brown eyes actually turned green."

"Oh!" said Kimmie. "I get it! That's why jealousy is called the green-eyed monster."

"Right," said Chloe, jabbing an elbow into Kimmie's side. "Now shush!"

"As the day of Zachary and Arabella's wedding drew near, horrible things began to happen around town. The pastor who was to unite them in matrimony, Pastor Puster —"

"Wait." Chloe giggled. "The guy's name was Pastor Puster?"

"Yes. Why?"

"It's funny. Never mind. Sorry, keep going."

"The week before the wedding, Pastor Puster was thrown from his horse and broke both of his legs. The women who were to prepare the food for the wedding feast all came down with smallpox, and the pretty little chapel where Zachary and Arabella would say their vows was infested with rats!"

"Rats?"

"Eww."

"Gross!"

"Was Martha the one making all these bad things happen?" Sam asked.

"They couldn't prove it, of course, but everyone knew it had to be her. And do you know what the punishment for witchcraft was in those days?"

"House arrest?" Alyssa guessed.

"Worse."

"Jail?" said Kimmie.

"Nope."

"What, then?" asked Chloe.

"Anyone deemed to be a witch was tied to a stake and burned alive."

At that moment, a log in the fireplace fell, causing a small burst of bright flames to erupt with a loud sizzle. The girls screamed.

"Did they burn Martha?" Chloe asked.

"They couldn't," Taylor explained. "They had a trial and everything, but no one could ever provide any hard evidence that Martha was the force behind the smallpox and the rats. Besides, according to the

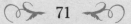

legend, Paster Puster was afraid to burn Martha. He believed that her wicked heart was so filled with envy and jealousy that if they burned her, the smoke itself would become infused with her wickedness and it would pollute the hearts and minds of everyone in Salem. He believed the only safe means of doing away with Martha would be to shoot an arrow through her evil heart at the precise moment that she was at the height of a jealous rage."

"Ouch!"

"Yeah."

"Wow."

"Of course, after the pastor made this proclamation, they found him dead in a meadow . . . with an arrow through *his* heart." Taylor shook her head sadly. "Poor Pastor Puster."

The girls were quiet, letting this all sink in.

"I sure hope this story has a happy ending," Sam said at last.

Taylor shrugged. "Well, they brought in a substitute pastor from another village to perform the wedding ceremony. Everyone figured that once Zachary and Arabella were married Martha would get the hint and just give up. And she did. Or so it seemed. For a few days, things were quiet. Then one day, an anonymous wedding gift was left on Arabella's doorstep. It was a beautiful bauble."

"A bubble?" said Kimmie.

"A bauble," said Taylor.

"What the heck is a bauble?"

"A little decoration," said Sam, "like a piece of jewelry."

"Why didn't she just *say* a piece of jewelry?" asked Kimmie.

"Shhhhh!" Chloe shot Kimmie a look.

The fire was dying, and the room had grown chilly; it was even more shadowy than it had been before. Taylor's voice seemed to tremble in the dimness.

"The gift was a lovely little crystal, and the note that came with it said that Arabella should always keep it near to her. The note said it would protect her. So the town blacksmith took the crystal and fashioned it into a pretty little necklace for Arabella to wear so she could be safe from rats and smallpox and crazy horses."

"I thought you said the Puritans weren't allowed to wear jewelry," Chloe reminded Taylor.

"They weren't," Taylor replied. "But this was a case of extenuating circumstances. The townsfolk were afraid Martha might start up with her tricks again, and since they didn't want to see Arabella get hurt, they made an exception, because everyone liked her so much."

"Boy," said Alyssa, "even back then it paid to be popular."

"So that's how it ends?" Sam prompted hopefully. "Arabella gets a good-luck charm and everyone lives happy ever after?"

Taylor bit her lower lip. "I'm not sure."

Chloe gasped. "You're not sure?"

"What do you mean you're not sure?" cried Kimmie.

Sam looked disappointed. "You're just going to leave us hanging like this?"

"That's as much of the story as I know," Taylor confessed. "I never actually heard the ending." She waggled her eyebrows and gave them a mischievous grin. "But I believe that Martha never really gave up on Zachary." She lowered her voice so that it was barely a whisper in the dusky room. "I believe that Martha's insatiable jealousy is still an evil force in this universe and that one day, she

will come back to wreak havoc on all who know her grim tale!"

At that moment, another log burst into flame just as the bedroom door slammed open!

"Ahhhhhhh!" everyone screamed.

The scream tore from Chloe's throat; she covered her eyes. Shrieking, Sam threw her arms around Kimmie and buried her head in her shoulder. Alyssa ducked beneath her sleeping bag.

"What's going on here?" came a snarky voice from the doorway.

Cautiously, Chloe lifted her head; for one crazy second she was convinced she would see Martha the witch standing in the bedroom doorway, clutching a dead rat by the tail.

But what she saw was just an older version of Taylor, with longer hair and a disgusted expression on her face.

"Guys," sighed Taylor, "this is my big sister, Jenna."

"You guys better not be getting nacho crumbs all over my bedroom rug!" snapped Jenna.

Kimmie immediately began sweeping up broken chips with her hands, but Chloe was so relieved that the intruder was just a bathroom-hogging,

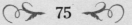

capri-pants-stealing big sister and *not* the ghost of Martha that she began to giggle. Sam joined in, then the others until they were all falling over each other in a giggling fit.

Jenna just rolled her eyes and shut the door.

CHAPTER SIX

Chloe was awakened from a deep sleep by the sound of groaning.

Or maybe it was moaning.

Whatever it was, it was a miserable sound and it was coming from Taylor's closet. Her heart pounded in her chest until she realized that the noise was probably just Kimmie. She'd eaten so much junk food, she'd probably given herself a big-time stomachache, and she'd crept into the closet so that her groans of pain wouldn't wake anyone.

"Too bad that plan didn't work," Chloe grumbled. Sighing, she threw back her warm sleeping bag and tiptoed across the room to see if Kimmie was okay.

The fire had long ago fizzled out, and the room was not only cold but pitch-dark. Chloe stepped over

the sleeping forms of her friends until she reached the closet door.

She opened it and stepped inside.

But Kimmie was nowhere to be seen.

What *was* visible was a tiny glowing light. At first Chloe thought it might be a night-light. Not that people usually kept night-lights in their closets, but Taylor was something of a fashionista. Maybe she kept a light on in here in case she got a sudden wardrobe inspiration in the middle of the night and had to rush in to put together an outfit without turning on the lights and waking Jenna.

But even groggy with sleep, Chloe knew that was a ridiculous explanation. Her heart began to thud again. She reached down and picked up the illuminated object from the ground.

It was Taylor's choker. And the crystal was shimmering and glowing as though it were on fire. As Chloe stood there, trembling, the crystal grew warm, then hot in her palm. Suddenly, there was a thunderous sound pounding in her ears, and her temples felt as though they were being pierced with red-hot daggers.

And then, a flash of brilliant light lit up the dark

little closet. Chloe gaped in horror as a ghostly image materialized before her. It was a beautiful woman, but she was screaming in agony. And no wonder! She was bound to a stake, and a ferocious fire raged around her. Chloe could actually feel the heat of the flames as she stared at the poor woman.

And then she saw it!

Around her neck, the woman was wearing a crystal choker.

Taylor's crystal choker! The very one that Chloe was holding in her hand.

Chloe pulled her eyes from the image and looked down at the crystal in her grasp. It shimmered, as though lit from within, and along with the light came a horrible howling sound. As the crystal vibrated against her palm, Chloe realized the moaning she'd thought was Kimmie was actually coming from deep, deep within the crystal!

As she gazed in horror at the choker, the light inside the crystal dulled and was replaced by a black, swirling cloud. From the depths of the cloud another image emerged — lips, contorted in a snarl, blazing red cheeks, and two big brown eyes. Chloe gasped as the eyes in the crystal locked on hers. For a moment the brown irises just stared at her, a dark gaze filled with evil. And then in a burst of sickening color and light, the brown eyes turned green!

"Martha!" Chloe cried in a strangled voice. "It's Martha!"

As she spoke the name, the crystal in her hand became so blistering hot that it seemed to sear her skin. With a shriek she flung the choker to the floor.

"Chloe!" breathed Sam.

"What's wrong?" Taylor cried.

"Are you all right?" asked Alyssa.

"What is it?" Kimmie shouted. "Speak to us!"

The noise in her head and the stabbing in her temples stopped as quickly as they'd come. Chloe turned to see her four friends huddled in the closet doorway. Their eyes were filled with panic and concern.

Mutely, she pointed to where she'd seen the woman burning at the stake just seconds before. But all she saw was Taylor's collection of jeans, sweaters, and dresses hanging innocently on the closet rod.

At her feet, the vintage choker lay on the carpet. She bent to retrieve it and held it out for her friends to see. "Look!" she cried, her voice hoarse. "Look at this!"

But the crystal was no longer groaning or glowing. It was just sitting there in the palm of her hand.

"It's a bauble," Kimmie remarked. "So what?"

Chloe blinked and shook her head. The image of the pretty woman tied to the stake was already fading from her memory.

"You must have had a bad dream," said Sam gently, putting an arm on Chloe's shoulder and guiding her back to her bedroll. "A really bad dream."

"Yeah." Chloe nodded, lowering herself to her sleeping bag. "Yeah, I guess I did."

"It must have been that stupid story I told," said Taylor. "I'm sorry."

"It's okay," said Chloe, settling back against her pillow. "I just want to go back to sleep."

She pulled the collar of her pajamas up around her chin and waited as her friends snuggled back into their own sleeping bags. When she was sure they'd all fallen asleep again, she carefully withdrew her arm from inside the covers.

There on the palm of her hand, right where she'd held the crystal choker, was a red mark that was beginning to blister. The kind of blister left behind after a really bad burn.

It was hours before she finally closed her eyes.

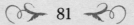 81

Chloe was the last one to awaken on Saturday morning.

Kimmie and Alyssa had left hours before; Kimmie had an early ballet class and Alyssa was going to visit her grandparents. Sam's mom wouldn't be picking her up till noon, to go to Davis's football game.

It was 11:55 when a very sleep-deprived Chloe padded into Taylor's kitchen. Sam and Taylor were already dressed and eating a late breakfast. The first thing Chloe noticed was that Taylor had put her choker back on. Seeing that crystal made Chloe's heart flip; she briefly considered darting back upstairs, grabbing her stuff, and running out the door at top speed, never to return. But that would be silly. The choker dream had been exactly that: a dream.

Well, technically, it had really been more like a nightmare.

"Look who's up!" chirped Taylor.

"Morning." Chloe yawned and managed a smile as Sam slid a plate of waffles to her across the table. "Thanks. These look delicious!"

It took Chloe three bites of waffle to realize that,

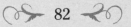

although Sam's backpack and sleeping bag were piled neatly in the corner of the kitchen, her signature fashion staple, the beloved jean jacket, was spread out on the kitchen table. It reminded Chloe of a patient about to undergo surgery on an operating table.

"What's this all about?" she asked, motioning to the faded jacket as she drizzled more syrup over her waffles.

"Sam's gonna let me glam up her jean jacket!" gushed Taylor.

"Glam up? What do you mean by 'glam up'?"

"You know," said Taylor, running her index finger along the collar of the jacket. "Embellish it. Trick it out! I was thinking I'd trim the cuffs and collar in sequins, maybe sew on some appliqués, or do a little embroidery with metallic thread. Stuff like that."

"I didn't know you could sew," Chloe remarked.

"Oh yeah! It's part of my whole fashion obsession. Which is why I'm so excited to get to work on Sam's awesome jacket."

Out of the corner of her eye, Chloe could see that Sam was smiling politely, but she looked a little wary. Chloe couldn't help wondering how much peer pressure Taylor had put on Sam to get her to agree to

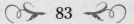

this project. After all, Sam's jacket was *sacred*! Adding sequins and "tricking it out" with a bunch of other glitzy junk seemed downright disrespectful.

Chloe turned to Sam, who shrugged.

"It might be cool to have something a little on the glitzy side for a change," said Sam, indicating her classic but simple Fair Isle sweater and khaki pants.

Chloe wished Sam sounded more confident in the plan. Before she could say so, Sam's mom was honking the car horn in the driveway.

"That's my ride!" said Sam, hopping up from the table. "Thanks for having me sleep over, Taylor."

"You're welcome. Thanks for coming."

"I'll text you later," said Chloe.

"Okay." Sam allowed herself one last, longing look at her unadorned jacket.

"Don't worry." Taylor gave her a reassuring smile and a pat on the shoulder. "I'll take good care of it, I promise."

With that, Sam gathered up the rest of her stuff and left.

As soon as the kitchen door closed behind Sam, Chloe cleared her throat.

"Um, Taylor. Can I ask you something?"

"Sure."

"That choker . . . has it ever *done* anything . . . weird . . . before?" As soon as the words were out, Chloe wished she hadn't asked. It was a ridiculous question.

"*Done* anything?" Taylor repeated. "How could it do anything? It's a choker."

"I know." Chloe blushed, feeling like a complete idiot. "Never mind. Forget I asked."

"No," said Taylor in a patient tone. "Obviously you're curious about something."

"Well, what I mean is . . ." Chloe sighed. "Last night, when I was dreaming or sleepwalking or whatever . . . your choker was in the closet, and I picked it up and it looked as though it were on fire!"

To Taylor's credit, she didn't laugh at Chloe's crazy statement. Encouraged, Chloe rambled on.

"I know it sounds nuts, but in the dream, the crystal was glowing, and there were, like, flames . . . *inside* it! And, well, I guess I was just wondering if that sort of thing ever happened to you when you were wearing it."

"No." Taylor shook her head. "Never."

Embarrassed, Chloe dropped her eyes to her sticky waffle plate. "That's what I thought."

But the heat that had emanated from the crystal in her dream had felt very real.

So real, in fact, that it could have left . . .

. . . *A scar!*

"But look!" said Chloe flinging out her hand for Taylor to see. "What about this?"

Taylor looked at Chloe's palm. "Ooh. That's a pretty bad burn."

"I know," said Chloe. "And I think . . . I think the choker did it. I mean, how else could I have gotten burned last night?"

Taylor frowned. "That's a good question."

"Right?" Chloe bobbed her head. "A very good question. Because I didn't go anywhere near the fireplace, and it wasn't a birthday sleepover, so there weren't any candles and . . ."

"What about the pizza? Remember how piping hot the pizza was when we started eating it? It was steaming when we opened the box! The cheese was all melty and drippy." Taylor gave Chloe a meaningful look. "And very, very *hot*."

Chloe thought back to their supper the night before. The pizza was so hot that even Kimmie had to force herself to wait to bite into it, and even then she'd burned the roof of her mouth on the super-sizzling cheese.

"Maybe some of the cheese dripped onto your hand and burned you," Taylor suggested. "Burns can be like that. They sting for a second, and then you don't feel them again until much later."

That was true. Once Chloe had burned herself taking a cookie sheet out of the oven, but she hadn't felt any pain until hours after, when it blistered.

"I guess you're right," she sighed, feeling silly, but also very relieved. "I guess that's what happened."

Taylor smiled. "Hey, I have a great idea!"

"As long as it doesn't have anything to do with hot pizza, I'm in! What's the idea?"

"Let's go shopping!"

Chloe didn't have to be asked twice. Gobbling the last of her waffles, she sprung up from the table and hurried upstairs to change.

CHAPTER SEVEN

Twenty minutes later Chloe returned to the kitchen, ready for a day of serious shopping.

At the bottom of the stairs she stopped dead.

"Ready to go?" asked Taylor. "Jenna's going to drive us into town."

But Chloe couldn't answer; she just stood there, stupefied, staring at Taylor.

Taylor frowned and planted her hands on her hips. "What now?"

"You're . . . you're wearing Sam's jacket!"

"So?"

So?

"So . . . it's *Sam's* jacket. She left it here for you to . . . whatdyacallit? Glam up. She didn't leave it here for you to wear."

"Chloe," Taylor sighed, "I would think you, of all people, would understand about the creative process. I mean, you're an *actress*."

Chloe couldn't see how being an actress had anything to do with Taylor wearing Sam's jacket. "What's your point?"

"My point is that before I start going all fashion-designer on this old thing . . ." Taylor tugged at one of the faded denim sleeves. ". . . I'll need to get a sense of the fit and the feel. To see how it wears, learn how it flows."

Chloe was skeptical. Sam had been wearing that jacket for years and had never said a single word about the "feel," let alone the "flow." "I don't know, Taylor. Samantha's really possessive about that jacket. I don't think she'd even let *me* borrow it."

But Taylor didn't seem to be listening anymore. She'd turned to check herself out in the hall mirror. Smiling, she flipped up the collar, and rolled up the sleeves. Then her hand went to her throat so she could adjust the crystal choker. "Why should Sam have a jacket like this when I don't?" she said huffily. "I want one. I deserve one. And it looks just as good on me as it does on her. Maybe even better."

Chloe watched Taylor's eyes flashing in the

mirror as she admired herself in Sam's jacket. *So much for feel and flow,* she thought. Taylor was wearing the jacket for one reason and one reason alone: because she wished it were hers!

With a pang of dread, Chloe followed Taylor out to Jenna's car.

Chloe didn't say much during their shopping expedition. As they wandered in and out of the many Main Street stores and shops, she watched silently as Taylor examined sparkly little stick-on beads and gems, fluffy marabou feather trim, and glittery appliqués. She studied iron-on patches, and fabric paint and metallic ribbons in a zillion different colors. In theory, she was shopping for items to glamorize Sam's jean jacket. In reality, she didn't purchase a single one of them.

After passing by four shoe stores; a jewelry store called Earrings, Earrings, Earrings; and a shop that specialized in imported sweaters, they arrived at Envy, the cool boutique where Chloe had purchased her doomed yellow cardigan.

Taylor's eyes lit up at the trendy fashions displayed in the window.

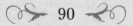

"Let's go in here!" she cried, tugging Chloe by the arm.

"Sure," Chloe grumbled.

Inside, Taylor browsed the racks and shelves, oohing and ahhing over scarves and jeggings, belts and hats. She tried on several silver bracelets and even pretended to be interested in a faux-diamond nose ring.

The salesgirl, with her long dark hair, perfectly made-up eyes, and stylish outfit, looked as though she'd just stepped off the cover of a fashion magazine.

"Can I help you with anything?" she asked Chloe and Taylor.

"You don't have any of those pretty yellow cardigans left, do you?" Chloe ventured.

The girl gave her a sad smile. "Sorry, hon. Those went like hotcakes when we marked them down last month." She turned her smudgy, smoky eyes to Taylor. "Hey, that is an awesome jean jacket."

"Thank you," said Taylor, a smug little lilt in her voice. "I've had it for years. It's my favorite."

Chloe's mouth dropped open in absolute shock.

"It fits like it was made for you," the sales-girl observed.

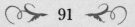

"Well, it kinda was," Taylor lied. "In fact, I had it custom designed. In Paris." Then, in case the salesgirl was a total airhead, she added in a pompous tone, "That's in France."

Chloe couldn't believe what she was hearing. That was Sam's jacket — the one she only washed in cold water with gentle detergent; the one she always took off before she ate anything with ketchup; the one she never wore on the school bus because the seats were grungy and she didn't want to get it dirty. This jacket was *not* from Paris (France!) and it was *definitely* not custom designed for Taylor!

"I was thinking about cutting off the sleeves," Taylor confided to the salesgirl. "Turning it into a vest. And maybe I'll tie-dye it."

"Awesome!" said the salesgirl, then went off to help a customer who was looking for a pair of lime green combat boots.

But Taylor's lies continued to echo in Chloe's head. "Taylor," she said evenly. "I think you should give me that jacket. Now."

Taylor whirled on Chloe so fast, and with such an expression of fury, that Chloe actually flinched.

"Why?" Taylor demanded.

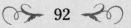

"Um, well . . . because I think Sam forgot that . . . that . . ." *Think fast, Chloe.* "Forgot that tomorrow the Kendalls are having their family portrait taken."

"So?" Taylor gritted her teeth. "What's that got to do with *my* . . . I mean, *this* jacket?"

"That's what Sam's wearing for the portrait!" Chloe fibbed. "The whole family is wearing them! Mr. and Mrs. Kendall and Davis and Sam . . . they're all going to wear jean jackets for the family portrait."

"Oh, really?" Taylor folded her arms across her chest and gave Chloe a challenging glare. "What are they, a motorcycle gang?"

"No!" Chloe forced a laugh. "No, of course not. It's just, ya know, one of those casual-type portraits. Real laid-back. And what's more laid-back than a whole family wearing jean jackets? In fact, I think they're going to be barefoot, too." She laughed again. "Those Kendalls! What a fun bunch."

After what felt like a thousand years, Taylor sighed and shrugged off the jacket just as the sales-girl returned. Chloe snatched it before Taylor could change her mind.

"How we doing over here?" she asked, then noticed Taylor's choker. "Great necklace! Hey, I've

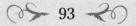

got some really great jewelry cleaner in back. If you'd like, I can take that and polish it up for you."

"Thanks," said Taylor, unclasping the choker and handing it to the girl.

"I should probably leave now," said Chloe, clutching the jean jacket. "I've got to get home."

Taylor looked confused. "You're leaving? I thought we were gonna go to Earrings, Earrings, Earrings. To buy some, ya know . . . earrings."

Chloe shook her head in disbelief. Two seconds ago, Taylor had been glaring daggers at her, and grinding words out through her teeth. Now she was heartbroken over the fact that Chloe wanted to go. What was up with that?

"And why are you holding Sam's jacket?" Taylor asked.

Um, to keep you from amputating the sleeves, that's why.

"Just because." Chloe shrugged and gave Taylor a weak smile. "Listen, we'll do Earrings, Earrings, Earrings another time, okay?"

"Okay. When?"

"When? Um, well, I guess when I need a new pair of earrings."

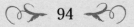 94

Taylor nodded. "All right. Well, I'll see you in school. And don't forget, the cast list for *The Crucible* is going to be posted first thing Monday morning."

"I won't forget. Bye, Taylor, and thanks for the sleepover." Chloe took the jean jacket and headed out the door.

Through the window of Envy, Chloe saw the salesgirl come back and hand Taylor her choker. For a second, she felt a little guilty about fibbing and about leaving Taylor to finish her shopping trip alone.

But then she remembered the look in Taylor's green eyes when she'd told those lies about Sam's jacket.

Suddenly, she couldn't get away from there fast enough.

By Monday morning, Chloe had put all the strange events of the weekend out of her mind. All she could think about as she hurried along the sidewalk toward school was the cast list. Mr. Wentworth had said he would post it outside the drama classroom right after homeroom.

Sam was getting off the school bus just as Chloe arrived.

"Hey!" Sam called, waving from the bus steps.

"Hey," said Chloe, handing Sam her jean jacket. When Sam gave her a puzzled look, she explained, "The jacket is perfect the way it is. I talked Taylor out of that whole glam business. I hope you don't mind."

"I don't mind at all." Sam grinned and hugged her jacket to her chest. "I never should have agreed to it in the first place. I was worried about it all weekend."

"Speaking of being worried . . ." Chloe took a deep breath. "The cast of the play is going to be announced this morning. Will you come with me to the drama classroom to see if I got a part?"

"Do you even have to ask?"

Her best friend's smile went a long way toward calming the racing of Chloe's pulse. "Meet me in the south stairwell right after homeroom."

"I'll be there."

Homeroom seemed to go on forever. When at last the bell rang, Chloe was out the door like a rocket. She met Sam and together they took the stairs two at a time.

A crowd was gathered around the drama class-room; the list was posted on the door.

"I'm too nervous," Chloe gulped. "Will you look for me?"

"Sure," said Sam. "Wait here." She shouldered her way through the throng of would-be actors toward the list.

Chloe felt someone come up beside her. She turned to see Taylor, who looked as anxious as Chloe felt.

"Well?" Taylor asked.

"Sam's looking now. She's going to let me know if —"

Chloe was interrupted by a hoot of absolute glee. It was a hoot she'd recognize anywhere.

"You got the lead!" Sam cried. She was jumping up and down, and pumping her fist in the air victori-ously. "Chloe, you got the lead! You're Abigail Williams!"

"Me?" Chloe gasped; her knees buckled as a jolt of pure joy shot through her. "I got the lead!?"

She turned to Taylor, who was smiling.

Well, sort of. The corners of her mouth had turned upward and her teeth were showing, so tech-nically, by definition at least, there was a smile on

Taylor's face. The problem was, there wasn't an ounce of happiness in it.

"How nice for you," Taylor said tightly.

Sam had pushed her way back through the crowd and flung her arms around Chloe. "Congratulations! You did it." Then she turned her beaming face to Taylor. "You got a part, too! You're playing the role of Mary Warren."

"Mary Warren?" Taylor's frozen smile turned to a frown. "That's a terrible part."

"No, it's not," said Chloe. "It's a good one."

"Not as good as Abigail Williams," Taylor spat, her eyes narrowing to slits. Almost immediately, her tight smile returned, and she said with forced brightness, "But that's okay! I'm sure I'll enjoy being Mary."

"Of course you will!" said Sam encouragingly.

Chloe wished she had some words of comfort for Taylor, who obviously felt disappointed at not getting the lead. But she was just so surprised and overjoyed by her own good fortune, she didn't want to focus on Taylor's distress.

Luckily, Taylor excused herself. "I'm going to the girls' room," she said. "I'll see you guys later." She turned and stomped off down the hall.

"See you," Chloe called after her, then as an after-thought added, "and congratulations."

Taylor kept right on stomping.

"What part did Jennifer Thomas get?" Chloe whispered to Sam.

"Rebecca Nurse," Sam reported. "I think that's a pretty big part. Not as big as Abigail, but still pretty good."

"Oh. Well, I guess she'll be happy about that," Chloe observed.

"No she won't." Chloe and Sam turned to see Amy, one of Jennifer's BFFs, standing behind them.

"But Rebecca's a really great part," Chloe said reasonably.

"That has nothing to do with it," Amy said, her eyes troubled. "Jennifer's not going to be in the play at all. In fact, she's not going to be in school for quite a while. That's why I'm here. Jennifer sent me to find out if she got a part, and if she did, I have to tell Mr. Wentworth to recast it."

"I don't understand," said Chloe, a weird churning beginning in her stomach. "Why can't Jennifer be in the play?"

"Something terrible happened on Friday," Amy

explained. "Jennifer had gym class, and afterward, she went into the showers, like usual. She brought the travel-size bottle of shampoo she always uses, and washed her hair."

Chloe still didn't see the problem.

"Someone tampered with Jen's shampoo!" Amy exclaimed, her voice trembling.

"Tampered with it?" Sam repeated.

Amy nodded, wiping tears from her eyes. "They mixed some sort of nasty chemical in with the shampoo. It totally destroyed Jennifer's hair. It's all burned and broken and fried, and it's turned this hideous shade of green!"

Chloe's hand flew to her mouth. "Oh no!" Her head swam with the horrible image of Jennifer's beautiful hair breaking off in chunks from some unknown chemical. "What is she going to do?"

"She had to cut it all off," said Amy.

Chloe felt absolutely sick to her stomach. All that beautiful blond hair . . . gone. It would grow back, of course, which was a good thing. But the whole thing was just so horrifying.

"Who would do such an awfully cruel thing?" Sam wondered.

Amy's face turned cold. "There's only one suspect."

"Who?" breathed Chloe.

"Drew Devlin!"

That sort of made sense. Drew Devlin and his twin brother, Dean, were the biggest troublemakers in school. They were supposed to be ninth graders but they'd stayed back twice, which was why they were in Chloe and Sam's pre-algebra class. Still, something as vicious as adding acid to someone's shampoo seemed extreme, even for the Devlins.

"Did he have something against Jennifer?" Chloe wondered.

Amy nodded. "He asked her to the Halloween dance last month, and of course she turned him down. But Jen was super polite. She wasn't mean about it or anything."

Chloe couldn't help herself; she gave Amy a skeptical look.

Amy sighed. "Okay, fine. She *was* mean about it. Jennifer can be pretty snippy when she wants to be, and she laughed in Drew's face. She said she could go with any boy in the whole school, so why would she ever go with a juvenile delinquent like him!"

That sounded more like Jennifer. But in her heart, Chloe knew that even a mean girl like Jennifer didn't deserve such brutal revenge.

"I should go talk to Mr. Wentworth," Amy said grimly.

"Tell Jennifer we hope she feels better," said Chloe, and she meant it.

When Amy was gone, Chloe turned to Sam. "I feel awful. I think I'm gonna go to the restroom and splash cool water on my face."

"I'll go with you."

As they turned the corner toward the girls' lav, they saw the door swing open and Taylor thunder out. She looked even angrier than she had when she'd left the drama room. Chloe considered shouting for her to wait up, but thought better of it and let Taylor stomp off down the hall.

Moments later, Chloe and Sam entered the bathroom . . .

. . . and they couldn't believe what they saw inside!

CHAPTER EIGHT

Trashed!

The second-floor girls' lavatory was completely and totally trashed.

Literally! Dirty, crumpled towels and other disgusting clumps of rubbish that Chloe didn't care to identify were strewn across the tile floor. It was obvious that someone had dumped out the filthy contents of the tall trash can, which now lay on its side in the center of the room. The can itself was so creased and bent that it looked as though a truck had driven over it.

"Whoa," breathed Sam, taking in the mess.

In addition to the garbage, there was a long, jagged crack in the mirror above the sink — Chloe guessed that whoever had dumped the trash out had

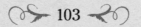

followed up that nasty act by hurling the heavy metal can at the mirror. A web of delicate fissures and fractures radiated outward from the big crack like a million silver scars. Two of the stall doors were severely dented as if they'd been pounded on or kicked in, and the third door had been yanked off its top hinge and now hung at a listless angle, swinging slightly back and forth like an injured limb.

Then there was the graffiti. Every cinderblock wall was defaced with angry slashes and scribbles made with a thick green marker. None of the writing was legible except for one word, scrawled in bold block letters across the shattered mirror:

ENVY

"Do you think whoever wrote that was referring to the fashion boutique?" Sam asked doubtfully.

Chloe shook her head. "If they were, then it's definitely what you call bad advertising." She frowned. "I think it's about real envy. You know, jealousy. The emotion."

"The only emotion I'm feeling right now is fear," said Sam. "So can we just get out of here?"

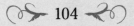

"Yeah, definitely. Let's go."

As Chloe followed Sam out of the restroom, she turned back to take one more look at the battered bathroom. She had the weird sensation that she could still feel the furious vibes of the vandal who had left the mess behind. In fact, it was as if there were an echo, not only a feeling but a sound. A ghostly voice, a whispered word, trembling eerily in the atmosphere: "*Arrraaaabellllllaaaa . . .*" it hissed.

With the hair prickling on the back of her neck, Chloe shut the door and left as fast as she could.

The note landed on Chloe's desk as though it had simply fallen out of the sky. Over the years, she and Sam had perfected their in-class note-passing skills to the point that not even their eagle-eyed pre-algebra teacher, Ms. Ford, could catch them at it.

Chloe unfolded the note and reread the entire exchange; Sam had written first:

I bet it was Taylor who trashed the bathroom.
You saw how mad she was about being
cast as Mary Warren.

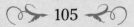

To which Chloe had replied:

She was mad, but I can't believe she'd do something so destructive.

Sam's answer came back lightning quick:

It <u>had</u> to be her! She was the last one to use the lav!!

Sam had a good point, of course. All evidence pointed directly to Taylor. Slowly and as discreetly as possible, Chloe turned to peer over her shoulder at Taylor, who was seated three rows behind her. Unfortunately for Taylor, she was flanked by the Devlin brothers; Drew sat to her left, Dean to her right. At the moment, Drew was using a ballpoint pen to carve his initials into the desktop, and Dean was tearing pages out of his textbook and folding them into paper airplanes. Taylor was just sitting there sulking.

Sighing, Chloe wrote another installment on the wrinkled note paper:

Are you going to tell on her? Check one:
_____YES   _____NO

She folded it into a tiny triangle then tossed it in a graceful arc in Sam's direction. It landed soundlessly on Sam's binder; Sam swept it into her lap just as Ms. Ford turned away from the board.

"We will be having a test at the end of the month," the teacher announced, eliciting a grumble from the class. "It will encompass everything we've covered this semester and it will be worth eighty percent of your grade. So I suggest you begin studying now!"

Chloe took out her pink highlighter and opened her binder to the assignments page. She made a note of the test, and underlined it four times, just as the bell rang. Her classmates gathered up their books and backpacks and shuffled out.

Taylor brushed by her without even saying a word.

Chloe was just tucking her highlighter back into her pencil case when Sam's response landed on her desk.

Are you going to tell on her? Check one:
_____YES   _____NO

  _X_ Maybe
Sorry, Chloe, but I just don't trust that girl.

With a heavy sigh, Chloe crumpled the note and stuffed it into her pocket. All things considered, she really didn't blame Sam at all.

By lunchtime, the entire cafeteria was buzzing about poor Jennifer Thomas. Some kids were saying the chemicals had been put into Jennifer's shampoo, others said it was her conditioner that had been tampered with. The craziest rumor had Jennifer tripping in the shower and getting all her hair sucked down the drain. It was hard to know what to believe since the school officials were determined to keep the details of the incident under wraps. The latest news was that both Devlin boys had been questioned extensively by the principal, the vice principal, and three different guidance counselors, but in each interrogation, the twins had vehemently denied having anything to do with it. In fact, Drew Devlin informed the administrators that he'd had an early-morning orthodontist appointment on Friday and hadn't even gotten to school until well after first period. He even offered to get a note from the orthodontist testifying to his whereabouts. Since there

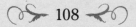

was no way to place either Devlin at the scene of the crime, neither received punishment.

Chloe was the first to arrive at the lunch table. She slid her tray to the far end and stared out the window, trying to make sense of all the weird things that had been happening. The creepiest, of course, was the dream she'd had in Taylor's closet, but what about the mini-attack in the west stair-well, Jennifer's tainted hair-care products, and the trashed bathroom?

"Hey, there she is!" Kimmie's excited voice floated into Chloe's thoughts. "The star of the Marblehead Junior High stage!"

"Congratulations!" Alyssa cried, placing her lunch bag next to Chloe's tray. "The lead! I'm so proud of you."

"We're all proud of you," Sam amended, slipping into the chair across from Chloe.

In spite of her icky mood, Chloe smiled. "Thanks, guys."

To Chloe's surprise, when Taylor arrived two seconds later she was smiling.

"Guess what? I have big news!"

"Let's hear it," said Alyssa as she unwrapped her

ham-and-cheese sandwich. "Unless it's more gossip about Jennifer and Drew."

"It's a little bit about Jennifer," Taylor said, "but mostly it's about me!"

Alyssa shrugged. "Okay, I can live with that."

"What's the news?" asked Kimmie.

"Well, we all know that that somebody put chemicals in Jennifer's herbal-citrus shampoo, right? And that she's going to be out of school for a long time because of it."

"Yeah," said Kimmie. "But what's it got to do with you?"

"Well, I'm going to be playing the part she was supposed to play in *The Crucible*. I'm going to be Rebecca Nurse." She struck a little pose and beamed at them. "It's the second-best female role!"

Four pairs of eyes just blinked at her.

"It's not that I don't feel bad for Jennifer," Taylor clarified quickly. "Because I do. I really do. But the show must go on, right? And somebody's got to play her part."

"Taylor's got a point," said Alyssa, biting into her sandwich.

"We're happy for you," Kimmie said.

"Yeah, congratulations," said Sam.

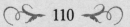

Chloe managed a smile, but said nothing. Something was nagging at the back of her brain, something that felt wrong about what Taylor had just said. She just wished she could put her finger on what it was.

She didn't get to think about it very long though, because Davis Kendall had sauntered up to their lunch table. She couldn't think about much of anything when Sam's brother was around. Under the table, her feet began to tap uncontrollably and her palms got so sweaty she was afraid the milk carton would slip out of her hand.

"What's up, Davis?" Sam asked. "If you're here to switch lunches with me the answer is no! Mom put the last pudding cup in my lunch because I called dibs —"

"Relax, Sammy, I don't want the pudding cup," Davis assured his sister. "I just wanted to come over and say congratulations to Chloe." He turned his crooked grin to Chloe. "Nice going, getting the lead and everything."

"Thanks." Chloe's feet were tapping so hard now she felt like a Radio City Rockette.

"I'm sure you'll be great as Abigail," Davis added. "My buddy Javier is going to be on the light crew and he said everyone's talking about how good you're gonna be."

Chloe felt her cheeks flushing, and there was a fluttery feeling in her stomach. But before she could thank Davis again, Taylor piped up.

"I'm playing Rebecca Nurse."

"Oh." Davis gave her a polite smile. "That's nice."

"I'm Taylor." She batted her green eyes and gave her red curls a purposeful toss. "I heard you were the star of your football game this weekend." She shook her hair again, clearly intent on making Davis the Fan of Redheads take notice.

"Well, it was a team effort," Davis said with a modest smile. "See you guys later."

When he was gone Sam gave Chloe a strange look. "Are you okay?" she asked.

Chloe's answer came out in a breathy rush. "Yes, I'm okay. Of course I'm okay. Perfectly okay. Why? Don't I look okay? Because I'm okay. Okay?"

"Oh . . . kay," said Sam. Then she gave Chloe the tiniest little smile and excused herself to go get another napkin.

And in that moment, Chloe knew. Chloe knew that Sam knew that Chloe had a crush on her big brother, Davis. And apparently, Sam didn't think it was weird at all.

Chloe had never felt so happy in her life. Until . . .

"Davis is a major hottie," Taylor observed in a thoughtful tone, twirling one red curl around her finger.

Chloe didn't like the sound of that.

"Well, *duh*." Alyssa rolled her eyes. "Everybody knows Davis is hunk-a-licious."

Baxter and Drake arrived then, all excited to report that they'd overheard some ninth graders saying that Drew Devlin had just challenged the vice principal to an arm-wrestling contest. Not only that, but there was a new rumor circulating that Jennifer had secretly agreed to go steady with Dean Devlin, which was why Drew had tampered with her shampoo in the first place.

The mention of Jennifer's shampoo set off that nagging sensation in Chloe's mind again. She felt as though she were on the verge of coming to some important realization when Taylor leaned over and whispered in her ear.

"I think I'm going to start flirting with Davis Kendall," she said.

Chloe opened her mouth to say something, but quickly clamped it shut. After all, what *could* she say? *"I forbid you to flirt with my crush, you backstabbing redhead."*

Okay, so it did have a nice ring to it, but maybe it wasn't a case of backstabbing at all. Maybe in all the excitement of the auditions and the sleepover and the Jennifer incident, Taylor had simply forgotten about Chloe's secret crush on Davis.

That wasn't the type of thing friends usually forgot about, but it was possible. And it sure beat the only other explanation, which was that Taylor was fully aware that Chloe was crushing on Davis and just didn't care. And if that was the case, the fact of the matter was that Chloe had no claim to Davis. He wasn't a pudding cup she could call dibs on.

Suddenly, Chloe's head was spinning, and the pleasant flutter in her belly had been replaced with a deep, dull ache. She stood up, grabbed her backpack, and glanced at Taylor. "I'm going to the library to study for the pre-algebra test," she snapped. "See you at rehearsal."

CHAPTER NINE

For the next three weeks, Chloe did her best to avoid Taylor.

Outside of rehearsal, pre-algebra, and gym (which they also had together), she tried to stay out of Taylor's orbit. During lunch, she'd make excuses to go to the library or meet with teachers for extra help. At rehearsal, she managed to keep her distance by talking to other actors or busying herself with the costume designers and sound techs. On weekends and after school, if Taylor invited her to hang out, Chloe pretended to have family obligations or too much homework. Unfortunately, this resulted in Chloe missing out on any activity in which Taylor included Kimmie, Alyssa, or Sam, but Chloe just couldn't shake the feeling that she should keep her

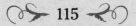

distance from Taylor. She might have been destroying her social life, but on the upside, all the extra library time and teacher meetings were certainly having a positive effect on her grade point average.

Sam seemed to sense that Chloe was purposely steering clear of Taylor, and although Chloe was sure Sam missed her, her best friend was sensitive enough not to complain. Sam and Chloe texted as often as ever, and got together outside of school when they could. But they were careful to keep these outings secret from Taylor. Since tonight was the Sunday night before the big pre-algebra exam, Chloe headed to Sam's house for their final study session.

"How's rehearsal been going?" Sam asked as they sprawled on the floor of Sam's room with their pre-algebra notes and textbooks.

"Great," said Chloe. "I love acting, and Mr. Wentworth says I'm doing a wonderful job. But it's also been a little bit weird."

"Weird how?"

"Well, last week when one of the techies was putting my body mic on me, something went wrong. There was this giant spark and I got a pretty bad electrical shock."

Sam gasped. "That's awful! You could have been really hurt."

"I guess. I mean, it all turned out okay. Joey, the ninth grader who's in charge of the sound crew, checked the microphone and said it was pretty ancient, like from the nineties, so there was probably just a short in the wiring. But Billy Tibbs and Madison Arnold were wearing body mics that were just as old and they were fine."

"Do you think someone tampered with your mic?" Sam asked in a worried tone. "Like what happened to Jennifer's mango–green tea shampoo."

"It was herbal-citrus," Chloe corrected absently. "According to Taylor, anyway." She sighed, her thoughts returning to the faulty microphone. "I suppose it's possible that somebody fooled with the wires, but I can't imagine who or why. Everybody's really excited about the play, and we all want it to be the best it can be. It wouldn't make sense for someone in the cast or the crew to sabotage me." She took a deep breath to get up the nerve to say what she was thinking. "At first, I thought maybe Taylor had something to with it."

Sam's eyebrows shot up. "Seriously?"

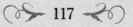

Chloe nodded. "I mean, she's been nice lately, especially at rehearsal. I guess she's in a good mood because of the whole costume thing."

"What do you mean?"

"Well, we spend a lot of time doing costume fittings and working on costume changes, and since she's so into clothes and fashion that really makes her happy." Chloe smiled. "I like it, too. When we put on our Colonial-era costumes, it's like we literally remove all reminders of our present-day lives. We take off all our regular accessories, like hair clips and watches and jewelry — Taylor even takes off that choker she always wears. And then we put on pinafores and mobcaps and petticoats, and it's like going back in time."

"Cool," said Sam.

"Yeah. And when we're in costume, Taylor is like the nicest person ever. She's focused and encouraging and really helpful. Like, for instance, yesterday when I went to the wardrobe closet, the dress I'm supposed to wear for the biggest, most important scene was torn."

Sam frowned. "Torn?"

"Yep." Chloe nodded. "The whole bodice was split

at the seams. I guess I was careless when I took it off the day before, although I don't remember hearing it rip. Anyway, since Taylor knows how to sew and stuff, she offered to take it home and repair it."

"That was nice of her, I guess," Sam allowed. "And what about last Wednesday in gym, when Coach Emerson made us climb the ropes? Coach told us it was unsafe to wear jewelry during the climbing activity, and she made Taylor take off her choker. Then I beat Taylor to the top of the rope by a mile, which I thought would really upset her, but she was actually really impressed and told me I did an awesome job."

Chloe remembered. It was like Taylor had two totally different personalities. At times she could be sweet and generous, and at others she could be a calculating, envious monster.

A green-eyed monster!

As Sam searched the pre-algebra handouts for their next practice equation, Chloe searched her own mind . . . trying to make some sort of connection between Taylor's weird changes in behavior. What was the common denominator between all her jealous rages?

She was distracted from her thoughts by the sound of the doorbell ringing downstairs.

Sam looked up from her notes, puzzled. "Who could that be?" she wondered. "Showing up at seven o'clock on a Sunday night?"

"Let's go downstairs and see," Chloe suggested. "I could use a hot cocoa anyway."

"Sounds good," Sam said, grinning. "But let's bring the textbook so we don't waste any precious study time while we're waiting for the water to boil."

When they got to the bottom of the stairs they nearly tripped over each other in shock. There in the Kendalls' living room, seated on the sofa beside Davis . . . was Taylor, in all her red-haired glory. Her backpack sat on the sofa beside her, and she was holding a small notepad. Chloe hated to admit it but Taylor looked dazzling in a fluffy chartreuse V-neck sweater that showed off her crystal choker. She was also wearing an extra-flouncy little skirt and the black leather designer boots that she'd told Chloe she only wore for special occasions.

Evidently, Davis Kendall was a special occasion.

"Taylor?" said Sam. "What are you doing here?"

Taylor looked up. When she saw Samantha and Chloe together her green eyes flashed. Maybe it had

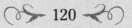

something to do with the mood lighting in the Kendalls' living room, but Chloe could have sworn Taylor's eyes looked even greener than usual.

"I have to write a sports article for my journalism class," Taylor informed them in a huffy tone. Her eyes were practically shimmering now, as green as Granny Smith apples. "So I came by to interview Davis about the football team."

Chloe shot her a skeptical look. "You could have just interviewed Drake and Baxter at lunch."

"I could have," Taylor said coldly. "But I didn't."

Of course she didn't. Because this so-called interview was a perfect excuse for Taylor to spend time alone with Davis. Chloe wondered if there even *was* a sports writing assignment. She rolled her eyes, heading for the Kendalls' kitchen. "Sure, Taylor. Whatever."

"Don't you 'whatever' me, Chloe Rawlings!" Taylor leaped to her feet. Her fists were clenched at her sides, and again those greener-than-green eyes flashed like neon. "You're supposed to be *my* friend," she shouted, pointing a finger at the textbook in Chloe's hand. "And yet, here you are studying with Sam. Why didn't you invite me?!"

"Because you do *this*!" Chloe shouted back. "It's

like every time someone does or gets or has something you want, you throw a hissy fit! You can be mean and sneaky, Taylor. You get consumed with jealousy, and it's creepy!"

As though to prove Chloe's point, Taylor let out a shrill scream and flung her little notepad across the room. Sam ducked just in time; the notepad sailed over her head and knocked over a china bud vase on the fireplace mantle.

Chloe stared in horror as the choker at Taylor's throat lit up with an eerie red glow. She flashed back to the night of the sleepover when she'd dreamed that the crystal had been burning from within.

A look of pain contorted Taylor's features as her hand flew to the glowing crystal against her skin; it was as though she were being scalded. In a frenzy of panic Chloe considered running to Taylor and jerking the choker right off her neck, but Taylor looked so terrifying that Chloe couldn't bring herself to approach her. Even Davis had begun to back away.

Now Taylor picked up her backpack from the sofa and hurled that across the room, too. Among the contents that spilled out was a fat green Magic Marker.

Images flashed in Chloe's mind: the girls' lav . . . the graffiti . . . ENVY. Sam's hunch had been correct: Taylor's fury over not being cast as Abigail was so great that she'd vandalized school property.

"I should have waited for you to get to the *top* before I dragged you down!" Taylor bellowed. "I should have waited until that fall could have done some real damage!"

It took a moment for Chloe to understand that Taylor wasn't speaking metaphorically. She was talking about Chloe's very real tumble down the steps of the west stairwell. It had been Taylor who'd grabbed her from behind and made her fall! But why? Had she wanted to eliminate her as competition for the role of Abigail?

Of course. And what about Jennifer?

The nagging little curiosity in Taylor's brain suddenly exploded into a full realization. When all the other kids had been guessing about which of Jennifer's hair-care products had been tainted, Taylor had said with complete confidence that it was Jennifer's *herbal-citrus shampoo*. But the school administrators had kept that detail classified. So how would Taylor know . . . unless she'd been the one to do the tainting!

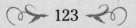

It made perfect sense. Taylor had been livid over the fact that Jennifer had such lovely blond hair. Add to that the possibility of Jennifer getting the role of Abigail, *and* the fact that Taylor knew Jennifer would be showering after gym on Friday morning (Jen had been complaining about the hot-water issue for all to hear) and Taylor became the number-one suspect!

Davis was gathering up the things that had fallen out of Taylor's book bag, including the incriminating green marker. With an expression of disgust he handed her the backpack and declared, "Interview over. Go home, Taylor."

"Fine," said Taylor. "I'll go and leave you two besties to study for the pre-algebra test all by yourselves. Have fun! I hope you both fail!"

Taylor ran out of the living room, slamming the front door behind her.

"She may not be a real witch, but she sure acts like one!" said Sam, going over to pick up the overturned vase. Luckily, it was still in one piece. "I bet that's why she had to leave Salem. No one who spends more than a few minutes with her wants to be her friend!"

Chloe knew Sam's comment was only a joke to lighten the horrible tension, but maybe there was something to what she'd said. Maybe the question of Taylor's crazy, jealous behavior did have something to do with her past.

And maybe Salem was where she'd find the answer!

CHAPTER TEN

On Monday, Chloe and Sam took their seats in pre-algebra, ready to tackle the big exam. Ms. Ford handed out the test and the room went silent except for the scratching of pencil points on paper.

About halfway through the exam, there was a knock on the classroom door and the principal poked his head in. Chloe struggled to concentrate on the test problems, but she couldn't help glancing up toward the front of the room, where the principal was whispering something to Ms. Ford. With wide eyes, the teacher began to riffle through her desk drawers, flipping through folders and even searching under her blotter. After a good five minutes of hushed conversation the principal left, and Ms. Ford stood up in front of the class. She looked ready to spit nails.

"Pencils down!" she said in a harsh voice.

Everyone obeyed immediately.

Tony Harris, a studious boy who sat in the desk next to Chloe, looked perplexed. "We still have time left," he pointed out.

"I realize that, Tony," said Ms. Ford. "But this test is being canceled."

A murmur of confusion rippled through the classroom. Chloe glanced over her shoulder at Taylor, who looked just as surprised as the rest of the class. It was then that Chloe noticed the desks on either side of Taylor were empty.

The Devlin twins were not in class.

"I am being forced to reschedule the test," Ms. Ford continued, "because I have just been informed that earlier today the answer key was stolen from my desk."

This revelation was met with a collective gasp. Someone stole the answer key? It was almost unthinkable! That was cheating. MJHS operated on an honor system, and every student signed the honor code on the first day of school; therefore cheating was punishable by suspension. "The answer sheet was found in the possession of two of the students from this class," Ms. Ford explained. Nobody had to ask who those two students were. The Devlins' empty desks, not to mention their reputation, said it all.

"To further complicate the situation," said Ms. Ford, her voice growing even more serious, "there is the chance that the perpetrators made a small number of copies of the answer key, which they may have distributed to other students. According to the honor code, anyone with information about this possibility should come forward immediately."

"What do you mean by information?" asked Tony.

"I mean," said Ms. Ford, "that if anyone here has any reason to suspect a fellow classmate of having received a copy of the answer key from the Devlins, they must say so."

That translated into tattling. And everyone knew it.

"How would we know?" Tony asked.

"Well," said Ms. Ford, "if, perhaps, you witnessed someone in the company of Dean and Drew Devlin — particularly someone who doesn't ordinarily interact with them — that would be a very incriminating sign."

When Taylor's hand shot up, everyone spun in their seats to stare at her.

"Yes, Taylor?" said Ms. Ford.

Taylor's eyes had changed from their usual bright emerald to a sickly, swampy green. "I saw Samantha Kendall with the Devlins!" she hissed.

There was another gasp of disbelief from the stunned students. All eyes turned to Sam, who had gone perfectly pale.

"Are you absolutely certain?" Ms. Ford asked Taylor. To Chloe's relief, the teacher looked as though she didn't believe the accusation. "This is a very serious charge."

"I saw Samantha Kendall with the Devlins!" Taylor repeated.

Sam was shaking in her seat; tears streamed down her cheeks. "No!" she said. "I didn't get a copy of the answer key from the Devlins or anyone else! Honest!"

Looking grim, Ms. Ford approached Sam's desk. Wordlessly, she picked up Sam's unfinished test paper and studied it.

The teacher's voice was soft and very sad when she said, "All of these answers are correct."

"That's because she cheated!" cried Taylor.

"No," Chloe countered, glaring at Taylor. "It's

because she studied! She studied like crazy, and so did I. Sam would never cheat."

"You can't prove that she didn't!" Taylor snarled.

"And you can't prove that she did!" Chloe shot back. "It's just your word against hers."

Ms. Ford was quiet for a long moment. "I'm sorry, Samantha," she said at last. "A test key is missing, and an accusation has been made. I will have to run this by the principal, and, of course, I will be calling your parents. But under the circumstances I think we will all be in agreement that you must be put on academic probation."

Chloe wasn't sure what that was, but it didn't sound good.

Then the class bell was blaring. Sam gathered up her things and ran out of the room.

"Leave your papers on your desks," Ms. Ford directed with a sigh. "I will let you know when the makeup test will be."

Chloe turned to Taylor, who looked wicked and smug. And that was when she noticed that the crystal on her choker was filled with swirling green smoke. And from deep within, Chloe could swear she saw two evil eyes staring out at her.

Chloe knew now more than ever that she had to get to Salem, and she had to get there fast!

After rehearsal that day, Chloe called home and told her mother she was staying late to help paint scenery. Then she called a taxicab.

Ten minutes later she was sliding into the backseat of a yellow sedan and telling the cabbie to take her to Salem. She'd borrowed money for cab fare from Kimmie, telling her she needed the cash to buy additional play tickets since she'd just found out her aunt and uncle would be coming down from Boston to see the show. She promised she'd pay her back first thing in the morning.

Chloe hated lying to her mother and her friend, but she had to figure out what was going on with Taylor.

The cab driver dropped her in front of the house where Taylor used to live, a stately old saltbox colonial. Chloe had found the address easily enough online by searching the real estate transaction records for Salem. Luckily, the people who'd bought it from the Dunbars still hadn't moved in yet; from the looks of things, they were having the interior

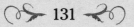

freshly painted first. A pickup truck loaded with ladders and paint cans sat in the driveway, and the front door was open.

Chloe took a deep breath and entered the house. It was empty of furniture; the floors were covered with color-spattered drop cloths, and the whole place smelled of turpentine and new paint.

"Hello?" she called. Her voice echoed through the unfurnished rooms.

"Up here," came a man's voice. Then a face poked over the upstairs railing. "Can I help ya, kid?"

"Um, yeah. My name's Taylor Dunbar. I used to live here."

"Yeah? So?"

"Well, I think I left something way in the back of my closet," she fibbed. "I was wondering if I could go look for it."

"Okay with me. Just don't touch the walls or the woodwork. Everything's still wet."

Chloe mustered a weak smile. All the lies she'd been telling were leaving a bad taste in her mouth. She left her backpack in the front hall and climbed the stairs.

At the top, she froze. Of the three bedrooms

off the second-floor hallway, she had no way of knowing which one had been Taylor's. After a moment's reasoning, she ruled out the largest one, figuring that had been Mr. and Mrs. Dunbar's master bedroom. But she still had to choose between the remaining two.

The painter noticed her hesitation. "Dontcha remember which room was yours, kid?"

"Oh, sure," said Chloe, gulping hard. "It's just that . . . uh, well, I have a big sister who's always taking my stuff, so this thing that I'm looking for could easily have been left in her room. I should probably check both."

The painter nodded, straightening his little paper cap. "Say no more, girlie. I've got a kid brother myself. He'd have stolen my dirty gym socks when we were kids, if I hadn't kept an eye on him." With that, the painter went downstairs to grab a clean brush.

Relieved, Chloe made her way into the first bedroom. It had a sloping ceiling and four small windows. She wished she knew what she was looking for; she could only trust that she'd know it when she saw it. She opened the closet door and found that it was completely bare. Not so much as a forgotten hanger or dented shoe box remained.

She crossed the hall and entered the next bedroom. This one had two small closets flanking the one large window, which had a cozy window seat beneath it. She peered into each closet, but again found nothing. Discouraged, she plunked herself down on the bench of the window seat.

It made a hollow sound.

It wasn't just a bench, it was a built-in storage chest!

Chloe sprang up from the seat and saw that it had a hinged top. Heart pounding, she lifted the lid.

For the most part, the storage chest was empty, but in the far corner at the back, Chloe spotted a paper bag. Reaching in (and hoping that there wouldn't be any spiders) she grabbed the bag, closed the lid, and hurried back downstairs.

When she got to the front hall, she found the painter holding her backpack and frowning.

"S-something w-wrong, sir?" she stammered.

"You said your name is Taylor Dunbar," the man said. "Then how come the name tag on your backpack says Chloe?"

Chloe let out a little squeal of panic. "Good question. Wrong house!"

She snatched the backpack, dashed out the front door, and ran as fast as she could until she'd rounded the corner and Taylor's old house was out of sight.

Only when she was sure that the painter wasn't following her did she stop to breathe.

And to examine the bag she'd found in the window seat.

It was just a little brown paper shopping bag, but there was a logo printed on the side: YE OLDE CURIOSITY SHOPPE, SALEM, MA.

Since it was the only clue she had, Chloe headed for Main Street.

When she arrived at Salem's quaint little shopping district, the sun had already set. It was dark and chilly as Chloe wandered from store to store.

Finally, she came upon a dusty little shop at the end of a shadowy old alley. The glass door looked to be older than Salem itself; it was warped and smoky with age. Painted on the wavy glass in

fading gold calligraphy were the words YE OLDE CURIOSITY SHOPPE.

"I guess this is the place to go when you're curious," Chloe muttered. "And I'm curious." Mustering her courage, she pushed opened the creaky door and stepped inside.

The tiny store was poorly lit and crowded from front to back and floor to ceiling with vintage clothing, old furniture and knickknacks, books, paintings . . . and jewelry. If there were ever a store that screamed "Taylor" this was it.

An old man sat on a rickety wooden stool behind the counter. For all Chloe knew he had been sitting there on that stool since Salem was inhabited by Puritans. She felt a wave of relief when the old man smiled at her. The fact that he reminded her of her grandfather gave her the courage to make her inquiries.

"A friend of mine has a necklace," she began, nearly gagging on the word *friend*. At the moment, she considered Taylor her worst enemy. "It's a choker actually. It's kind of jangly, made of some sort of metal, and it has a big, shimmery crystal in the middle. Is there any chance she bought it here?"

The old man nodded, his eyes darkening in a way that made Chloe think she might have frightened him with her description. "Sounds like Martha's Madness," he said slowly.

"Martha's Madness?" Chloe repeated; the name was ringing a bell, but she couldn't quite place it.

"That's what the locals called it. That little choker dates back to the 1600s. Legend has it that the necklace was once believed to possess dark powers." The man sighed. "I had it here in my shop for years. Truth be told, I was glad when it finally sold. Thing gave me the willies, it did."

Chloe felt a surge of hope; she was getting close to solving this creepy mystery. "Did you sell it to a girl about my age by any chance?"

"I did, in fact," said the shopkeeper. "I tried to talk her out of it, at first. I even tried to tell her the awful story of Martha and Zachary . . ."

The story! The scary one Taylor told them at the sleepover! Now Chloe knew why the name Martha sounded familiar. So this is where Taylor had heard the story. It seemed weird that she never mentioned that the story had been about her very own choker! And what was even weirder was that she hadn't known how it ended.

"What do you mean you *tried* to tell her?" Chloe asked.

The old man shook his head. "I got as far as the part where Arabella received the anonymous gift. But your little friend was in a hurry and couldn't stick around to hear the rest of the tale."

"I've got time," said Chloe.

The old man settled himself more comfortably on his stool. "Well, Arabella was thrilled with her pretty little necklace. She wore it all the time, and everyone commented on how lovely it was. But then something strange began to happen. Arabella, who'd never seemed to have an envious bone in her body, started behaving like a jealous shrew. Whenever her husband, Zachary, so much as tipped his hat to another lady, Arabella would fly into a jealous rage. If her neighbors happened to come into possession of a new workhorse, Arabella would insist that Zachary buy her two new stallions, just to show them up. If the neighbors bought two additional acres of land, Arabella ordered Zachary to acquire four additional acres, so as not to be outdone." The old man shrugged. "You get the picture."

"What happened to her?" Chloe breathed.

"Well, folks at the time tended to blame anything they couldn't explain on witchcraft. It was wrong, of course, and ignorant, but that was just how it was back then. And since no one, not even Zachary, could explain this new side to Arabella, the town elders declared that she must be evil and sentenced her to death."

"Oh no!"

"Poor Zachary was heartsick, of course, because despite her jealous ways he still loved her. He cried out that he must have something by which to remember his beloved. The elders took pity on Zachary, and they let him remove the choker from her neck. And in that moment, everything about Arabella changed. All the jealousy and wickedness just disappeared, as though it had been magically removed from her soul."

"It was the choker!" Chloe cried. "The choker made her jealous."

The old man nodded. "Come to find out, that nasty Martha had sent Arabella the anonymous gift, but not before casting an evil spell on it. Martha wanted to get revenge on the woman who'd won Zachary's heart, and she thought the best way to do

that was to make Arabella suffer the same intense jealousy Martha herself had known."

"Did the elders charge Martha with witchcraft then?" Chloe asked, riveted by the tale.

"They couldn't. Before the constable could grab a hold of Martha, she called upon the powers of darkness to save her. And they did! In a swirl of green mist, Martha disappeared — vanished completely so all that was left was the choker. For years it was on display in the town meetinghouse, just to remind the citizens of the power of evil. Some believed that Martha had escaped by hiding inside the crystal, but most people thought that was just plain silly. Eventually, they realized there was no such thing as witchcraft, and they lost interest in the choker. The way I hear it, Arabella's grandchildren ended up selling it in order to buy a new cow or something like that. After that it was passed down through generations as nothing more than a piece of antique jewelry."

And three centuries later an innocent seventh grader bought it, totally unaware of the age-old hex that turned her into a green-eyed monster every time she put it on.

"Thank you for the information," Chloe said to the shopkeeper.

"You're very welcome," said the old man. "Now, can I interest you in a set of commemorative Salem witch trial salt and pepper shakers?"

Just to be polite, Chloe bought an I ♥ SALEM bumper sticker and a little plush black cat that meowed when you squeezed its tail.

Then she called another taxi.

On the ride home, she came up with a plan.

CHAPTER ELEVEN

The next day in the girls' locker room, right before P.E. class, Chloe prepared to test her theory about the hexed choker causing Taylor's jealous fits.

She waited until Taylor had changed into her gym clothes and had taken off the necklace before she approached her.

"Hard to believe there are only two more days till opening night!" she said, being careful to sound as though nothing unusual had been happening.

Taylor gave her a glowing smile. "I know! I'm so excited!"

"How's that torn dress coming along?" Chloe asked.

"Oh, it's terrific," Taylor replied, sounding utterly sincere. "It won't be done in time for dress rehearsal

tomorrow, but I'll definitely have it ready for opening night."

"Great," said Chloe. "Because I really want it to look good. After all, I am the *lead*." Chloe made sure to emphasize the word *lead*. She wasn't used to bragging, and acting so self-important made her uncomfortable. But it was all part of the plan, and she had no choice but to go through with it.

"Don't worry," said Taylor. "You'll look amazing."

They made their way out of the locker room and into the gymnasium where Coach Emerson was setting up the free weights and explaining to the girls about muscle tone. When Sam spotted Chloe talking so pleasantly with Taylor, she looked surprised. Actually, she looked betrayed. But Chloe sent her a look that said, *Trust me*, to which Sam responded with a quick little nod. She may not have known exactly what Chloe had up her sleeve, but their friendship was solid enough that Sam had faith in whatever it was Chloe was up to. With a tiny smile, Samantha went back to doing bicep curls.

"Thanks again for mending the dress," said Chloe, turning back to Taylor and the wardrobe topic. "I'm really glad you'll be able to fix it. I think it's the *best* costume in the whole show, don't you? Better than

anyone else's. And it I think it looks really great on me."

Taylor bobbed her head up and down enthusiastically. "Absolutely. That high collar and those starched cuffs! Puritanical fashion at its finest! And I love the embroidery on the apron."

"I bet you wish you had a costume like that," Chloe baited.

Taylor sighed. "Well, sure, it would be nice to have such a cool costume. But a dress like that would be all wrong for my character."

Chloe smiled inwardly. No flashing eyes, no seething words, and, thankfully, no ten-pound dumbbells being thrown across the gym.

The real Taylor was, as Chloe had suspected all along, a nice, normal, non-insanely jealous girl.

It was just her *jewelry* that had a bad attitude!

Chloe texted Sam that night and asked if they could walk to school together the next day.

As they made their way up Old Burial Hill, only a few shafts of pale winter sunlight were peeking through the gnarled gray tree branches along the horizon; behind them, Marblehead Harbor lay cold

and dark, looking bottomless in the morning gloom. In the stillness of the early hour, Chloe told Sam her theory about Taylor's jealousy and the story of Martha's Madness.

"That's just so incredibly bizarre," said Sam. Her breath formed a tiny cloud, a frosty ghost in the frigid air.

Chloe nodded. "I know."

"And I can't believe she pulled you down the stairs!" Sam looked angry. "You could have been really hurt."

"I know that, too." Chloe's stomach lurched as she remembered her near miss in the west stairwell. "But it's not her fault. Not that or trashing the lav, or ruining Jennifer's hair." She paused. "Or getting you in trouble with Ms. Ford."

"Yeah, that." Sam sighed, her brow wrinkling. "You're sure she was acting under the influence of a curse when she did it?"

"Positive. When I talked to her in gym yesterday, I said all these boastful things to make her jealous. I was totally trying to instigate a hissy fit. But she wasn't wearing the choker, so she was fine."

They trudged upward in silence for a moment. "Listen," said Chloe when they reached the top of

the hill. "I'm gonna put an end to this stupid curse once and for all. I just need two more days. And if after tomorrow night Taylor is still a cold, calculating, envious, green-eyed monster, then I promise, we'll never hàng out with her again."

"It's a deal," said Sam. "Do whatever you have to do. But please, Chloe, be careful." A look of concern passed over her face "Hexes and black magic and wicked spirits trapped inside crystals. What if crazy old Martha doesn't like your plan to save Taylor?"

Chloe's voice was serious. "It's a chance I have to take. Not just for Taylor's sake, but for everyone else's safety. If I don't . . . well, who knows what she'll do next."

They were standing at the edge of the old burial ground now; a sudden wind blew through the dying grass that fringed the ancient tombstones.

Maybe for old time's sake, or maybe just to be on the safe side, both girls drew in deep gulps of the icy morning air and held their breath.

That afternoon (with the minor exception of Chloe's costume still being out for repairs), dress rehearsal went off without a hitch. The lighting cues, the props,

the set changes — everything went as smoothly as if the show were being performed by a professionally trained acting company instead of a junior high school drama club. Mr. Wentworth was delighted with everyone's work and told them so; then he commanded that all the actors go home and get a good night's sleep so they'd be well rested for Thursday's opening-night performance.

The stage crew, however, would be working long into the night. Construction of much of the larger scenery was still incomplete, and the set builders were waiting in the wings to finish the job as soon as rehearsal was over.

As Chloe left, she could hear Mr. Wentworth's voice booming through the auditorium: "Will a stage-crew member please do something about the roof of John and Elizabeth Proctor's homestead? It's completely off-kilter!"

Chloe was waiting in the main lobby for her mother to pick her up when Drake and Baxter appeared, fresh from football practice.

"Hey, Chloe," said Baxter. "Waiting for your ride?"

"Yep. How about you?"

"My dad's driving us home," said Drake. "He's over in the auxiliary gym finishing up some Booster

Club business. The new archery equipment was delivered today. He's taking inventory of all the targets, and the bows and arrows."

"And the quivers," Chloe added, grinning.

"And the quivers!" Baxter laughed. "Ready for the big show?"

"Ready as I'll ever be," said Chloe, smiling. "I hope you guys will be there."

"Wouldn't miss it for the world," said Drake.

"Me neither," said Bax. "And, um, hey, Chloe . . . would you maybe do me a favor?"

Chloe was surprised to see that Baxter's cheeks were suddenly turning pink.

"Sure, Bax," said Chloe. "What is it?"

"Well, could you . . ." Bax was looking down at his sneakers. "Could you tell Samantha that . . . um . . . that I'd like to sit with her at the play?"

"Of course I will!" Chloe said, beaming.

Then Drake's dad arrived to collect the boys.

"How did the archery inventory go?" Drake asked.

"Not bad," his father replied with a chuckle. "Except with those bows and arrows all over the place, it looks like Robin Hood's band of Merry Men are holding a rummage sale in the auxiliary gym!"

Then Drake's dad wished Chloe good luck in the play, and he and the boys headed for the parking lot. A moment later, Chloe's mom's car pulled up. Evie was already in the passenger seat, so Chloe had to slide into the back; she was surprised to see that there was a shiny silver gift bag waiting for her.

"What's this?"

Evie turned around in her seat but Chloe couldn't read her expression. "It's from me."

Curious, Chloe dug into the puff of pink tissue and reached into the bag. A swell of warmth filled her as she pulled out a brand-new yellow cardigan that was even softer and prettier than the old one. And pinned to it was a gorgeous little gold bauble: a delicate pin in the shape of a star.

"That's for getting the lead," said Evie, smiling. "I always knew my little sister was a star!"

CHAPTER TWELVE

Chloe supposed it was normal to be nervous on opening night. But her nerves had nothing to do with lines or blocking or even wardrobe malfunctions.

What she was worried about was dealing with a powerful curse and possibly coming face-to-face with the evil spirit who cast it three hundred years earlier.

She went over the plan a thousand times in her mind, organizing her thoughts by typing out a step-by-step list using the notes feature of her iPhone.

1) Text Taylor and ask her to meet me backstage a half hour before call time. Give the excuse of wanting to try on my mended costume in advance.

2) When she changes into her Rebecca Nurse costume, swipe the choker from her dressing room.

3) Smash the crystal. Smash it good. Smash it into smithereens!

4) Keep my fingers crossed and try not to pass out from fear.

5) If smashing the crystal destroys Martha's spirit, then get on with the show.

6) If smashing the crystal DOESN'T destroy Martha's spirit, re-read item #4.

7) Run!!!!!

When Chloe got to the theater, she was glad to find that no one else was there. The stage was dimly lit and she could see that the efforts of the set builders had really paid off. The scenery was complete and looked terrific, including the Proctor homestead's roof, which now sat at a perfectly symmetrical angle. Chloe took a seat on the edge of the stage and waited.

She didn't have to wait long. Taylor arrived moments later.

She swept onto the stage, her face set in a stern expression. Chloe wished the lighting were better so she could see Taylor's eyes and gauge their greenness.

"I'm here," Taylor snapped, shrugging off her coat. "As requested."

The first thing Chloe noticed when Taylor took off her coat was that she was wearing the choker. The second thing she noticed was that she was wearing Chloe's dress.

The costume she was supposed to have mended and was bringing early for Chloe to try on. Taylor was wearing it herself.

The question, of course, was why?

Chloe wished she could consult her iPhone, but she was pretty sure she hadn't covered this eventuality in her plan.

"That's my costume," Chloe said.

"Not anymore it's not." Taylor's voice was an unfamiliar croak echoing through the empty auditorium. It sounded old and wicked and far away. Was it Martha's voice? Was she speaking for Taylor now?

Number four: Keep my fingers crossed and try not to pass out from fear.

"What exactly are you saying?" Chloe asked, pushing her shoulders back and trying to look brave.

"I'm saying I've decided I'm going to play Abigail Williams tonight," came the dark voice again. "That part should have been mine from the beginning. So instead of just fixing the split seams of this dress, I completely remade it. Altered it to fit me and me alone."

"So you're saying it's a custom-tailored colonial frock," Chloe joked, hoping to coax the real Taylor out. "And not just some cheesy off-the-rack Pilgrim design?"

Taylor just scowled at her.

Clearly, Chloe's plan was no longer in play. If Taylor didn't go into the dressing room and change, Chloe wouldn't be able to snatch the choker. She was winging it now.

Winging it . . . wings . . . she had an idea!

"Taylor, listen to me!" said Chloe, slowly backing up toward the wings. "This isn't you. A curse is making you jealous and mean!"

"I am going to play the lead," Taylor croaked. "You can be Rebecca Nurse! But I'm going to be the one taking the final bow."

Chloe took another step backward and another. Then she shuffled back just a tiny bit farther until she was almost in the wings. Slowly, carefully, she reached behind her . . .

"Do you hear me?" Taylor cried, her voice growing shrill and piercing the silence of the empty theater. "I am going to be the star, and I'm going to take that all-important final bow."

"Oh yeah?" Chloe's hand grasped a dangling rope. "Well, how do you feel about a curtain call?"

Chloe gave the rope a firm tug; down came the heavy velvet curtain, right on Taylor! It knocked her off her feet, burying her in a puddle of heavy fabric. Taylor grunted, her arms flailing, grabbing, as she tried to free herself from the weight of the curtain, but Chloe dodged her.

It was only a matter of moments before Taylor would be on her feet again, and Chloe had to think fast. Gathering her courage, she reached for Taylor's throat. Her fingers closed around the choker. With one good tug, the ancient metal of the necklace broke apart and the choker came away in Chloe's hands.

For a moment, Chloe just stood there, gripping the cursed choker. She hoped that taking it off Taylor's neck would be enough, that the curse would cease to affect her like it had the other times she'd gone without the necklace.

But one look at Taylor's face, contorted with fury and jealousy, told Chloe that this time it was going to be different. The power of the curse was now strong enough to control Taylor even if she wasn't wearing the choker.

Chloe felt the blood drain from her own face as she watched Taylor untangle herself from the curtain and rise to her feet.

"Give. Me. My. Choker!" she growled.

Chloe struggled to remember everything Taylor and the old shopkeeper had said about Martha; maybe there was something in the story that would give her a clue as to how to overturn this wicked curse once and for all: *Arabella, Zachary, the anonymous gift* . . . Her memory spun with images from the story: *the rats, the smallpox, Paster Puster* . . .

Suddenly, Chloe knew what she had to do. She turned and ran!

She could hear Taylor's footsteps behind her; her labored breathing echoing in the empty corridors.

When Chloe reached the door to the auxiliary gym she flung it open and burst inside. High windows at the top of the small gym let in only enough moonlight for her to see a short distance. She found what she was looking for just as Taylor appeared in the doorway.

"The story you told us about Martha and Arabella," said Chloe, "it's all true. But there was more to it than what you knew. Martha put a curse on Arabella, and she did it with this choker."

"You're just jealous because you don't have one!" Taylor spat.

Chloe almost laughed. Taylor was calling her jealous? If Chloe weren't so terrified, she would have cracked up.

"You got mad every time someone had something you wanted," Chloe explained, trying to keep calm as she backed slowly and steadily toward one of the archery targets. In the dim light she could barely make out the concentric circles of black, blue, and red, with the yellow bull's-eye at the center. "But it wasn't your fault, it was the curse of the choker."

Taylor, who was stalking toward Chloe with a fierce glint in her demon eyes, actually paused.

"But I should have had the lead role," she said.

"Everyone's entitled to her opinion," Chloe said with forced ease. As she spoke, she reached over and used the choker's broken clasp to fasten it to the center of the archery target. Then she lifted the bow and arrow she'd been holding and aimed it at Taylor.

Pastor Puster had said the only way to destroy the witch Martha would be with an arrow shot through her heart at the pinnacle of a jealous rage. So maybe the only way to end the curse would be to destroy the choker at the exact moment that the victim of the curse was at the height of her own jealous rage.

"Let's face it, Taylor," said Chloe, her voice taking on a superior air as she forced Taylor to back away from the target and the choker, "I'm just a better actress than you are!"

"No!" Taylor snarled.

"And Jennifer has way better hair than you do, and Sam and I are better friends than you and I will ever be! How does that make you feel?"

Taylor's answer was a roar of such hatred that Chloe's knees actually buckled with fear. But she didn't falter. She turned and aimed at the target. . . .

Hoping that this part of her plan worked out better for her than it had for Pastor Puster, she released her grip and let the arrow fly!

The tip of the arrow collided with the heart-shaped crystal. The sound it made was an earsplitting shatter, combined with the blood-curdling echo of Taylor's shrieking. It was almost as if the arrow had pierced Taylor's own cursed heart.

"Taylor!" Chloe cried. "Taylor, are you all right?"

Taylor fell to her knees, clutching her chest. Chloe's own heart was pounding as she turned from Taylor to the splintered charm hanging in the middle of the target.

She watched in amazement as a swirl of green fog rose from the shattered remains of the cursed choker. A writhing, slithering mist rose up from the shards of broken crystal, enveloping the auxiliary gym. And then, with a sound like thunder, the fog seemed to explode, vanishing into nothingness.

Chloe stared in horror at the empty place on the target where the necklace had hung moments before. Only the arrow remained, stuck in the bull's-eye.

Now Chloe ran to Taylor, who was no longer writhing in pain.

"Taylor?"

Taylor lifted her face to Chloe. Chloe's heart thudded with relief, because Taylor's expression was no longer wrinkled into a mask of jealous rage and envy. Instead, it was a face filled with confusion and fear. When her eyes met Chloe's, Chloe realized that for the first time in days she wasn't looking into the wicked, glittering green eyes of a cursed soul, but into the pretty, sparkling green eyes of a good friend.

"What happened?" Taylor asked.

Chloe let out a long rush of breath. "Let's just say I owe the Booster Club a really big thank-you!"

She dropped the bow to the floor and helped Taylor stand. "I promise to tell you all of it later. But right now, I believe we have a show to put on."

"Okay." Taylor nodded. "Um, Chloe?"

"Yes?"

"Why am I wearing *your* costume?"

Chloe laughed. Relief seemed to flood her from the top of her head to the tips of her toes. "It's kind of a long story," she said, smiling.

As they made their way back to the auditorium, something occurred to Chloe.

"Hey, Taylor."

"Yes?"

"The next time you go shopping for accessories, will you do me a favor?"

"Sure. What?"

Chloe draped a friendly arm on Taylor's shoulders. "Just skip Ye Olde Curiosity Shoppe and go to the mall like everybody else!"

CHAPTER THIRTEEN

The applause was deafening!

Peeking out from the wings, Chloe could see her mom and dad and Evie in the front row, beaming with pride. Behind them sat Alyssa, Kimmie, and Drake, and behind them were Sam and Baxter. Eyes shining with the satisfaction of a job well done, Chloe made her way to the center of the stage, and together she and Billy Tibbs took their final bow. The entire audience rose to their feet, whooping and whistling.

Above the thunderous din, Chloe heard a voice shout out, "Way to go, Chloe!"

It was Davis.

Chloe felt like she was glowing as the entire cast raised their hands to indicate the lighting crew in the upper booth at the back of the auditorium, then they swept their arms toward the orchestra pit where the stage hands had come out to be recognized. Finally, the whole cast joined hands and, with Chloe and Billy front and center, took one triumphant, collective bow.

As the curtain fell (for the second time that night, although nobody else knew that) Chloe felt a tug at her heart. It was over. In one shining moment of joy, the play had come to an end. And deep in her heart, Chloe knew that despite the complications, the confusion, and the curses, it had been one of the best experiences of her life.

It was a postperformance tradition for the actors and their friends to go out for ice-cream sundaes to celebrate. Mr. and Mrs. Rawlings waited for Chloe to change into her street clothes, then drove her to the ice-cream parlor.

"We'll come back for you in an hour," her mother said, her eyes still glimmering with tears of pride. "You did a wonderful job tonight, Chloe!"

"Thanks, Mom."

In a state of complete joy, Chloe made her way in to the ice-cream shop. Kids called out "congratulations" and "great job" as she passed, and Jennifer's friend Amy even offered Chloe a high five.

A high five from one of the popular eighth graders! Could this night get any better?

Apparently, it could . . . because the next thing Chloe knew, Davis Kendall was standing beside her.

"You were amazing, Chloe!" he said. "You really stole the show."

Chloe felt herself blushing all the way to her fingertips. "Thanks, Davis."

"What arc you having?"

"Um . . ." Chloe glanced up to the giant chalkboard above the ice-cream counter where all the flavors and specials were listed. "A hot fudge sundae sounds good," she said. "But then again, strawberry swirl in a waffle cone would be delicious . . ."

"Have both," said Davis with a huge grin. "You earned it!"

Chloe giggled. She was certainly hungry enough to polish off two ice creams.

"By the way, it's on me," said Davis, his voice suddenly shy. "That is, if you don't mind."

"No." Chloe's stomach did a happy little somersault. "I-I don't mind at all."

"Good," said Davis, his blue eyes sparkling. "Because I'd really like to treat you to some ice cream."

"Thanks. And just the one sundae will do."

Davis pointed to the far corner of the shop, where Sam and the others had already secured a large booth, and told her he'd bring over her ice cream as soon as it was scooped, topped, and ready.

Chloe nodded (because she was speechless) and had to force herself not to skip across the ice-cream shop to join her friends.

She dropped onto the pink vinyl banquette, looking a little dazed. "Guess what! Davis is treating me to ice cream!"

The girls smiled.

"Well, duh," said Sam with a giggle. "My brother's only been crazy about you since like forever."

"Now you guess what," said Kimmie. "Baxter is buying Sam her ice cream! And Drake is buying me mine!"

Chloe glanced at Alyssa, afraid she might feel bad that no boy had offered to buy her a sundae.

"Oh, don't worry about me," said Alyssa with a

big smile. "I'm just waiting for Billy Tibbs to arrive. He and I already have plans to share a banana split."

"He offered to treat you to a banana split?" said Chloe, surprised. Despite all his dramatic ability and stage presence, Billy was one of the shyest boys in school.

"No." Alyssa rolled her eyes. "I offered to treat him to one. And he said yes! This is the new millennium after all. If I want to buy the boy a banana split, I'm gonna!"

The girls burst into giggles.

Then Sam and Chloe filled Kimmie and Alyssa in on the rest of the story of Martha and her cursed choker. Chloe finished by telling them all about the standoff in the auxiliary gym, and the bow and arrow and her perfect shot.

"I guess you could say I got to the heart of the problem," she quipped.

That was when Taylor approached the table.

"Hi," she said, looking nervous, her eyes on Sam. "Samantha, I want to apologize about what happened in pre-algebra. It's all still a little fuzzy, but I'm beginning to remember stuff and I just want you to know how sorry I am."

"It's okay," said Sam. "It wasn't your fault."

"It was Martha's," said Alyssa.

Taylor shrugged. "I guess. But I feel bad. I was thinking I should probably turn myself in to the principal and tell him I was the one who trashed the bathroom and tampered with Jennifer's shampoo."

The others didn't think this was the best idea. Chances were the principal would never believe Taylor's supernatural tale about being under a jealousy spell cast by a three-hundred-year-old witch. Even if it was the truth!

"I have an idea," said Chloe, remembering the "anonymous gift" part of the Martha legend. "If you feel like you need to make amends for the broken mirror, you can contribute an anonymous donation to the school. People donate money all the time like that, and nobody ever cares where it comes from."

"That's brilliant," said Taylor with a big smile; but in the next moment her face fell again. "But what about Jennifer?"

This was a much tougher problem. The girls discussed it and together decided that the nicest thing Taylor could do would be to send Jennifer a gift certificate to a really posh beauty salon in Boston where their high-paid hair-care experts would know exactly what to do for her damaged hair. It wasn't a perfect

solution because she could never really apologize and of course the gift certificate would have to be anonymous, too. But the important thing was Taylor wanted to make up for the harm she'd done, even if she hadn't meant to do it.

They could see Drake, Baxter, and Davis on their way over to the table with the ice cream, and Billy Tibbs had just walked into the shop. Alyssa excused herself to join him at the counter.

As Davis approached with Chloe's sundae she slid a questioning glance toward Taylor.

"You okay with this?" Chloe whispered. "You're not jealous because Davis is buying me ice cream?"

Taylor laughed. "Not even a little. I'm so done with that."

"Good," said Sam. "Because before you got here, someone was asking about you. He said he'd like to be introduced."

"Really?" Taylor's pretty green eyes lit up with curiosity. "Who?"

Sam motioned to an adorable blond boy standing by the counter, holding a pistachio ice-cream cone. "Jake Bailey!"

With a little squeal of joy, Taylor went over to say hello to Jake.

Sam gave Chloe a look. "You're frowning. Don't tell me you're not happy about Taylor and Jake."

"Oh, I'm very happy," said Chloe. "I just wish . . ."

"Wish what?"

"That the ice cream he's eating wasn't *green*!"

They cracked up, and were barely able to settle down when the boys arrived with the ice cream. As everyone dug in, Chloe plucked the bright red cherry off the swirl of whipped cream and said, "I was wondering what you guys would think about something."

"About what?" asked Kimmie, wiping a smear of butterscotch sauce off her chin.

"About me joining the JV archery team!" Chloe tossed the cherry into her mouth and grinned. "Because something tells me I'd be a total natural!"

POISON APPLE BOOKS

The Dead End

This Totally Bites!

Miss Fortune

Now You See Me...

Midnight Howl

Her Evil Twin

Curiosity Killed the Cat

At First Bite

THRILLING.

BONE-CHILLING.

THESE BOOKS

HAVE BITE!

Accidentally Fabulous

Accidentally Famous

Accidentally Fooled

Accidentally Friends

How to Be a Girly Girl in Just Ten Days

Ice Dreams

Juicy Gossip

Making Waves

Miss Popularity

Miss Popularity Goes Camping

Miss Popularity and the Best Friend Disaster

Totally Crushed

Wish You Were Here, Liza

See You Soon, Samantha

Miss You, Mina

Winner Takes All